GINA CHUNG

Green Frog

Gina Chung is the author of the novel *Sea Change* (Vintage), which was longlisted for the Center for Fiction First Novel Prize and was a *New York Times* most anticipated book. A Korean American writer from New Jersey, Chung is a 2021–2022 Center for Fiction/Susan Kamil Emerging Writer Fellow and a recipient of the Pushcart Prize. She holds an MFA in fiction from the New School. Her work appears or is forthcoming in *One Story*, *The Kenyon Review*, *Catapult*, *Electric Literature*, *Gulf Coast*, *Indiana Review*, and *The Idaho Review*, among others. She lives in New York City.

ALSO BY GINA CHUNG

Sea Change

Green Frog

Green Frog

Stories

Gina Chung

Vintage Books
A Division of Penguin Random House LLC
New York

The Library of Congress Cataloging-in-Publication Data
Names: Chung, Gina, 1989– author.
Title: Green frog / Gina Chung.
Other titles: Green frog (Compilation)
Description: New York : Vintage Books, a Division of
    Penguin Random House LLC, 2024.
Identifiers: LCCN 2023020414 | ISBN 9780593469361
    (trade paperback) | ISBN 9780593469378 (ebook)
Subjects: LCGFT: Short stories.
Classification: LCC PS3603.H8534 G74 2024 |
    DDC 813/.6—dc23/eng/20230508
LC record available at https://lccn.loc.gov/2023020414

Vintage Books Trade Paperback ISBN: 978-0-593-46936-1
eBook ISBN: 978-0-593-46937-8

Frog by Steve Walker

vintagebooks.com

Printed in the United States of America
1st Printing

For 엄마, my first storyteller

. . . *let us have magic. Let us have*
our own mothers and scarves, our spirits,
our shamans and our sacred books. Let us keep
our stars to ourselves and we shall pray
to no one. Let us eat
what makes us holy.

—EMILY JUNGMIN YOON, "SAY GRACE"

Contents

Green Frog

How to Eat Your Own Heart

Step 1: Draw the water into a stainless-steel or copper pot. What it's made of isn't that important; what is important is that the pot be made of a material that you can dimly catch your own reflection in, the faintest outline of your face peering back up at you before the small blue flames on your stovetop warm the water into motion. But resist the urge to look closely, to trade your pot for a mirror, as that is not what you are here to do.

Step 2: Add sea salt, more than you think you will need. Scatter the crystals into your hand and throw them into the water, as though they are rice and you are the only guest at the world's smallest and saddest wedding. Stir until the salt dissolves, becoming a ghostly veil. Repeat until the water tastes like the sea, so salty it burns the inside of your mouth, scrapes your throat, makes your taste buds shrivel. Avoid watching the pot, because waiting for the expected to happen is energy you no longer need to expend. Walk away if you must.

———

Step 3: Once the water comes to a rolling boil, lean over the pot and feel its hot steam kiss your face. Whisper to it the names of your mother, your aunts, your grandmother, until it knows everything you know, steeped in the women who have come before you, who taught you this recipe and have perfected it over the years to ease their own heartaches—through wars and ghosts and children born dead and faithless husbands and family members never seen again. If you don't know your grandmother's name, don't call your mother to ask. Instead, remember that being able to know the first names of your elders is a luxury; speaking them aloud, even if to yourself, is a small heresy.

Step 4: Your knife should already be sharpened. If it isn't, hone the blade against a stone, the edge of a plate, a nail file. Remember that a dull knife is more dangerous than a sharp one— a sharp knife is biddable, easy to wield, but a dull one can turn on its master as quickly as a starving dog. You'll know you're done when the blade whistles through the air. Do not hold it like you are afraid, or it will dance out of your hands and cut your fingers to ribbons, until red pearls over your scarred wooden cutting board, staining everything.

Step 5: Chop scallions, ginger, and garlic into half-moons, crescents, slivers. Allow any stray pieces to fall from your cutting board and onto the floor. Lick the sticky acidity of the garlic off the blade of your knife, and let it bloom in your mouth like an earthy flower, until the metallic taste of your own fear is gone.

Step 6: Cut an onion in half. Remove the root and its papery jacket and the translucent layer inside. Bury the root in a plot of earth or keep it in the back of your freezer for stock, because what can be used again should be saved, as your grandmother once told you. Cut each hemisphere of the onion into three parts, using one hand to steady it and the other to slice. If your eyes smart, angle your tears into the pot, making the brine of your body useful for once.

Step 7: Aim the knife at yourself, your breastbone. Slowly, carefully, use the tip of the blade to trace a large circle around your nipple, cutting through the fat and tissue until your flesh opens like a door. From there, it will be easy to pull your heart out of its socket. Remember all the times you would have eagerly traded away this small, aching bundle of valves and ventricles for nothing more than a look, a promise, the touch of a hand. Be glad that no one ever took you up on your offer. Hinge your chest closed again. Sew up the wound with kitchen twine, or one of your own hairs. A safety pin, held in place and attached to the fabric of your shirt or apron, will do in a pinch.

Note: You may feel a small jolt once your heart has exited your body, but pay it no mind. Remind it that you've been through worse, like the time a boyfriend left you on a crowded train in another country during an argument, or the time a dining chair in your childhood home sailed across the room to strike the wall behind your mother, propelled by your father in one of his rages. A blade parting the surface of your skin is nothing, nothing.

Step 8: Plunge your heart into the boiling water the way you would a lobster. But there is no danger of your heart trying to escape, to scrabble at the sides of the pot in a desperate bid for freedom. Your heart is no crustacean, no hardy beast reared and shaped on the ocean floors over years of evolution. It is tender, foolish, easily shocked into submission. After five minutes, remove it from the water and plunge it into an ice bath. Stroke its rounded shape with one finger, like it is a spooked fish, or a bird that refuses to fly, until its wild beating stills.

Step 9: Heat a pan with a thin, neutral oil such as canola, sunflower, grapeseed (but if you only have year-old olive oil from the back of the grocery store, that will do). Throw in the scallion, garlic, and ginger slivers, and watch as they meet, negotiate with one another, alchemize. When the garlic begins to brown, add your heart to the mixture. Toss in your onion slices and allow them to caramelize, the salt and water of their membranes turning into something sweet. Set a lid on top and wait.

Step 10: Pour yourself a glass of whiskey. Pour yourself another glass of whiskey. Dip a cloth into the dregs of your glass and use it to clean your hasty sutures. Tell yourself you'll redo them tomorrow, restitch the wound in tinier, neater lines. Place your hand over the new hollow of your chest and try to guess how much your heart will shrink with the heat, how its seams and joins will sink into one another.

Step 11: Once your heart is fork-tender, serve it over a bed of sticky rice on your mother's best plate, the one with the hand-painted border of blue flowers and vines. Slice your heart into careful strips, long lines of red and purple. Douse them in soy sauce and vinegar. Chew every part at least ten times before swallowing. Your mother always told you to eat slowly, said it was good for digestion, for regulating the clockwork of the body. Feel each piece, each tendon, each vein slide down your gullet like silk, like a magic trick. Afterward, leave the dishes in the sink, the leftover blood marbling the stainless steel.

———

Step 12: Over the next few months, the remnants of your heart will grow inside your stomach, gestating like a child or a secret. Feel it remake itself, becoming once more a four-chambered, fist-sized, plump-veined creature of sound and motion. In the meantime, avoid alcohol, loud parties, flashing lights, shoes that constrain, mirrors that mock. Buy a dress for an occasion you don't have yet. Buy an expensive scented candle for no reason. Buy ten candles, ignoring your mother's voice in your head saying that you are literally burning money, and light them all at the same time, simultaneous bursts of frangipani and cinnamon and orange and gardenia and tobacco filling your room as if it were a confusing hothouse. Set a five-dollar bill on fire, just to see what it feels like. Instantly regret it and skip dinner. Paint your room, paint your hair, paint your face, until you no longer recognize anything in the mirror.

Step 13: When your new heart is ready, it will kick, rudely, against the walls of your stomach. Brace yourself, squatting in the bathtub, and pull it out from between your legs, slick with movement and heat and blood. It is so alive. Finally, cry while you unsuture the circle of skin around your breast and slip it back inside the house of your body. Listen as it stutters and starts, like an orchestra tuning up. Lie down in the tub, the back of your neck sweaty against the cool of the porcelain, as it fibrillates, thumps, begins again.

Green Frog

On the morning of the three-year anniversary of our mother's death, my older sister, Anne, calls to tell me she's two weeks late.

"I haven't taken a test or anything yet, though," she says, out of breath from power-walking down the avenues of Manhattan.

Anne is the kind of person who tracks her steps and sleep patterns and has had her entire life planned out since she was twelve, but she has terrible taste in men. She and her husband finally separated a few weeks ago, so this whole pregnancy thing couldn't have come at a worse time, even though, unlike me, Anne has always wanted to be a mother.

She asks me if I'm still in bed, and I lie and say no. She tells me that I should call her coworker, someone named Nadia who's looking for a roommate, because twenty-five is too old to be living at home with our father. That I have to start making healthier choices for myself.

I take down the number she rattles off to me, even though I am not all that interested in making healthier choices for myself. After I hang up, I get dressed while, out of habit, I avoid looking at the pile of discarded sketchbooks in the corner of my bedroom.

I dropped out of art school four years ago, in my junior year, when my mother was first diagnosed with stomach cancer. I told everyone I was taking a leave of absence to take care of her, but the real reason I left was that I couldn't stand being at that school, where everyone was so much more talented than I was. What I mean is, I wasn't bad, but I wasn't very good. Plus, the dean's office had sent me a letter, saying that I was going to lose my scholarship and that I would be put on academic probation if I didn't start doing better. Leaving felt like a relief, in a way. I knew I had never belonged there. The whole four-hour bus ride from Massachusetts to New Jersey, I stared out the window, avoiding my reflection and thinking about how I would tell my mother that I'd fucked up again.

A year later, she was gone.

My father is sitting in the living room with his Bible when I emerge from my bedroom. The TV mutters a televangelist's testimony.

"I thought we could pray today before we open the restaurant," my father says.

"Why?" I ask, not looking up as I pick through the piles of bills on our kitchen table.

"It's important that we commemorate this day with prayer."

I notice that he can't even say the words "your mother," and my nails bite into my palms.

"I have to go, Appa," I say. I let the door slam shut behind me.

It's pouring outside. An alert pops up on my phone: "Hurricane Warning this location till 9:00 PM EST. Avoid flood areas." Small lakes are already forming in the streets. I've forgotten my umbrella, and within five minutes I'm soaked. A car drives past, the reflection of its headlights luminous on the wet pavement. It's the kind of rain that reminds me of a Korean fairy tale Umma used to tell me when I was little.

She would begin the story in the same way each time: "A long, long time ago, there lived a green frog who always did the exact opposite of what his mother asked. If she asked him to go to the market to fetch rice, he'd go down to the valley and take a nap. If she told him to stay near the river, he would go up to the mountains."

"Was he bad?" I'd ask.

"Yes, he was not a very good boy," Umma would say, looking at me pointedly. "Driven to despair over her son, the frog's mother eventually became very, very sick. When she knew her time had come, she called him to her and said, 'When I die, bury me on the banks of our river.' She did this thinking he would bury her in the mountains, where her body wouldn't wash away."

Sometimes Umma was so tired from working at the restaurant that she would fall asleep in the middle of the story. "But he didn't do that?" I'd prompt her.

"No, he didn't." She'd rouse herself. "When his mother finally died, the green frog was filled with regret. He decided to do, for once in his life, the exact thing she had asked. Instead of burying her on higher ground, he buried her on the riverbank. Every day, he worried that the river would overflow and wash his mother's body away, and one day, during monsoon season, it did. He cried and cried, and that is why frogs croak in the rain."

Umma used to call me a green frog because, she said, she could never get me to listen to anything she said or do anything she asked. "Anne was never any trouble," she used to say to customers at the restaurant. "But this one. She always has to do things the hard way."

Umma said I came into the world fighting it. They had to induce my birth a week after my due date, because I didn't want to be born. "When you finally came out, your arm was thrown over your face, like you couldn't even face the world," Umma said.

Sometimes, when I was little, I would forget how to breathe, and my lungs would feel hotter and thinner by the second, like balloons that were expanding too quickly. The only thing that helped was when Umma held my face in her hands and stroked my eyebrows, reminding me to slow down and count my breaths. "You're here," she'd say. "And I'm here."

The year I started high school, my father left our family to be a missionary for four years, taking most of our savings with him. He told Umma he had heard the voice of God commanding him to travel the world and spread the word of His kingdom. They fought about it almost every night before he left. Anne and I dealt with it in our own ways—Anne by continuing to get excellent grades and throwing herself into ten new extracurriculars, and me by cutting class to smoke with my friends in the school parking lot or draw weird shit in the art room.

After Appa left, Umma took over managing the restaurant. She had me help with seating customers, taking orders, and cleaning the kitchen and bathrooms after we closed, but Anne was never expected to work at the restaurant, because she was too busy with orchestra or debate team. "Your sister has to study," my mother would say, as if Anne was the chosen kid, the one who would make all of Umma's sacrifices worth it. I started doing everything sloppily and slowly, hoping Umma would notice and stop asking me to help.

One night, a difficult couple complained that their galbijjim was too salty. Instead of offering to send their dishes back, I said that if they had a problem with our food they could just leave and not come back. "I should have known better than to ask you to help," Umma said. She told me to stay at home from now on.

During her last weeks in the hospital, Umma was high on painkillers all the time. I drew her hands, over and over again—in repose, resting on top of the covers as quietly as a doll's; her fingers interlaced with one another; her upturned palms, worn as smooth as old paper. I made each sketch as big as I could, her hands taking up the whole page like a bird's wingspan. I used charcoal, which left heavy smears on everything I touched, and I woke every morning with smudges like bruises all over my face and arms.

No one tells you how long dying takes. How much pain the body can endure before it finally shudders to a stop. How you can actually see, if you look closely enough, the breath of a soul leaving the body. I read somewhere that when someone dies you have to open the window so the soul can find its way out, but when I tried to open the window at the hospital, I found that it was sealed shut. For weeks, I had nightmares about windows and doors that I couldn't open.

"Jenny-yah," Umma said to me one night, near the end. Anne and my dad were asleep in the waiting room, and I was sitting alone by her bedside.

"Umma?"

Her lips were cracked. She moved them, but no words came out.

"Umma," I said, my eyes filling, "I'm sorry I messed up. I'm going to get myself together, I promise. I'll go back to school. I won't let you down."

"Green frog," she said, her eyes wide open.

When I get to the restaurant, I see that Thomas is already outside, locking up his bike. He nods at me, water angling its way down the brim of his cap. "Cancel your plans. Doesn't look like anyone's going anywhere tonight," he says.

"What plans?" I try to roll my eyes, but I'm too busy trying not to blush. Thomas is somewhere in his thirties and has huge, sinewy arms, covered with tattoos and burns. He has deep-set, tired eyes and a voice like gravel that makes heat rise inside my body, from my stomach to my face. It's a welcome distraction from the fact that nothing else is going on in my life.

My mother was the one who'd hired Thomas and the rest of our kitchen and waitstaff, planned and updated menus, and haggled with vendors over prices. But she let my father decorate, which was a mistake. The first thing you see when you walk into the restaurant is a backlit photo of Niagara Falls hanging above the register. The tablecloths are coral, so everything is tinged pink, like a slow algae bloom. There's a glowing fish tank by the register with a giant goldfish named Tubby. Umma won him in a church raffle a few years ago and fell in love.

I'm flipping the sign on the front door from "Closed" to "Open" when Tubby catapults himself out of his tank. He lands with a wet thunk on the floor and flip-flops across the tiles. I try to cup him in my hands, but it's like trying to hold on to a bar of soap that panics when you pick it up. Thomas helps me trap him and carefully slides Tubby back into the water.

"I guess he's gotten too big for that tank," I say.

"Maybe he just needs a friend to keep him company. Or maybe he needs to get out more," Thomas says.

"He's a fish, Thomas."

My phone buzzes with four texts from Anne. Three of the four messages are pictures of various pee sticks. The window on each test shows an unmistakable pink cross. The fourth message says, "Don't tell Appa yet. I'm coming by after work." To my surprise, I feel a soft flicker of something like excitement before I brush it aside to prep for the day ahead.

Almost all of our customers nowadays are people from my parents' church who feel sorry for us. "It's good to see children staying at home to take care of their parents," they say, their smiles as bright and flimsy as tinfoil. "What would your father do without you?"

There are so many things I'd like to say to that question. But I just thank them and stretch my lips across my face in my best approximation of a smile.

It's 5:00 p.m., when the restaurant is emptiest, when Mrs. Pak, who runs the flower shop next door, walks in. She has dyed rust-red hair, and when she laughs, she throws her head back so far you can see her gold fillings flashing. She's been coming by with pounds of marinated, freezer-ready meat and Saran Wrapped Tupperwares of stew since Umma's funeral.

"Is your father in?" She never says hello. She hands me the bags she's holding, and they are so heavy the plastic straps cut into my hands and around my wrists. "You're a good girl to help him out. But shouldn't you be working now, somewhere in the city, like your sister?"

"I'm happy to help here, Mrs. Pak. Thank you for all this, you're too kind."

"Oh, it's just some doenjang-jjigae and banchan I made the other day. You make sure to eat a lot too, so you can grow. You've always been so small, just like your mother."

I ask her if I can bring her some tea, because she is already taking off her raincoat and shaking her umbrella dry. She asks me to bring her coffee instead. When I come back with her coffee, she is examining our plants. "You need to repot these," she says. "I'll do it for you tomorrow."

"You don't have to do that, Mrs. Pak."

"Nonsense. Your father doesn't know the first thing about plants, and neither do you." She sips her coffee and sighs, rolling her neck.

Mrs. Pak's husband died about three years ago in a bad car accident on Route 17, and her son, who was about Anne's age, died soon after, of brain cancer. It spooks me to think about how many bad things can happen to one family, how much one person can lose in such a short amount of time. I remembered thinking after Umma died that the worst thing I could ever imagine happening had happened. I can't imagine having it happen twice.

The door jingles, and we look up to see my father. "Mrs. Pak, you shouldn't have come out in this weather," he says.

"I've seen worse storms. But perhaps we can all have dinner together. I brought you some food," she says, smiling at him.

I notice that he smiles back.

We've decided to close the restaurant, since no customers are coming in this rain, when Anne walks in, drenched despite her umbrella and impossibly chic designer raincoat. I take Mrs. Pak's containers into the kitchen, and Anne follows me.

"I didn't realize Mrs. Pak was going to be here. Is she interested in Appa or something?"

I shrug.

She imitates me, slouching and shrugging, which annoys me. She laughs. "Relax, I'm just teasing. Did you call Nadia about the apartment?"

"I have to be here to help Appa out with the restaurant."

"Appa is fine on his own. I think the only reason you're here is because you're scared to go anywhere else. Umma wouldn't have wanted you to stay here forever."

"Whatever," I say.

"You could go back to school, or get a job doing something you'd actually like or be good at for a change." Anne looks at me like all of this is so easy.

"I'm not like you, okay? The only thing I'm good at is disappointing people." I unlid each container and breathe in the comforting smells of garlic and spice.

"Jenny, you dummy. The only person you need to worry about disappointing is yourself."

We are not the kind of family that hugs. But when Anne wraps her arms around me—hesitantly, as though I am a wild animal with its leg caught in a trap—it doesn't feel uncomfortable. I close my eyes. She smells like an expensive garden. I try not to think about what I must smell like, and just focus on the feeling of what it's like to be held by my sister, to feel her arms anchoring me.

Later, after Anne has detached herself from me to go talk to Appa and Mrs. Pak, I watch the rain, its small hands drumming against the windows. It seems as though it will never stop. I lean over the sink and breathe on one of the windows, then draw a face with my finger. Two eyes, a nose, a mouth. I wonder what the baby will look like.

My father and I push a few tables together to make one large enough to seat all of us. Mrs. Pak heats up her doenjang-jjigae, and Anne plates the banchan—kimchi, tiny pickled anchovies, and acorn jelly with scallions and red-pepper flakes spooned on top.

I watch Thomas make kimchi pancakes, pouring the batter into a sizzling pan and frying perfect golden disks that we'll dip in soy sauce and vinegar. "The trick," he tells me, "is to wait until you see evenly spaced bubbles in the batter, like this. See? That's when you know it's time to flip it." He shows me how, doing it in one deft motion. "That's how your mom used to do it," he says. His hands, huge and knife-scarred and covered in stick-and-poke tattoos, look so different from Umma's, which were small and slim-fingered, but Thomas once told me that he'd never seen anyone debone a chicken or clean and gut a fish as fast as she could.

My father insists on praying over the food, so we join hands and bow our heads. He keeps it short, mercifully, and then we eat.

Mrs. Pak's doenjang-jjigae doesn't taste like my mother's, but it's earthy and comforting, with just the slightest hint of spice. I am ravenous, and I eat and eat until my belly grows swollen and tight and I have to unbutton the top button of my jeans. But I continue to eat. I'd forgotten how good it feels to be hungry, and to have that hunger satisfied.

Afterward, I look around at my father, Anne, Mrs. Pak, Thomas. No one really says much, which Umma always said was the sign of a good meal. We push back our chairs, rest our hands over our bellies. And even though we're done eating, no one moves to clear the plates yet, or to get up from the table.

The lights go out, plunging us into darkness. My breath gets short, and I feel the hot-air balloon feeling inside me again, but a moment later, they come back on. Everyone murmurs with belated surprise and then laughs, and I feel something inside me unclench.

I think about what Anne said, about how the only person I need to worry about disappointing is myself. About how my mother said that I always needed to do things the hard way.

About how maybe it's time to try something new for once, even if I don't know what it is yet, before it's too late. I could call that Nadia. I could start drawing again, enroll in an art class.

I am here, I remind myself. And maybe it's time I did something about it.

After the Party

The party was over. Mia Chang, thirty-six and in the first flush of what would, in a few years, become a full-blown midlife crisis, stood over the kitchen sink, surreptitiously smoking a cigarette out the window. From their bedroom down the hall, she heard her husband, Peter, mutter something in his sleep and sigh.

It had been a successful evening. Many of the guests were other math-department faculty members and their wives. It was surprising, Mia thought, though perhaps not too surprising, that almost all of the women at these gatherings were the wives, rather than faculty themselves. In his eagerness to make sure everyone had a good time, Peter had drunk too much.

Mia was loading plates into the dishwasher and gathering bottles for the next day's recycling when her mother called, at 1:00 a.m. She let the phone ring a few times and lit another cigarette, willing her heart to stop thudding so loudly, before she answered.

"Umma?" she said, trying to sound nonchalant. "What are you doing up so late?"

The refrigerator hummed impatiently. The kitchen was lit by a single light, the bulb over the stove. The nicotine coursing through her body made the light seem to pulsate.

"Your father finally moved out. He took everything. Even the loafers I gave him that he never wore."

Mia wiped away the purple circle of a wine stain on the scratched kitchen counter. "Well, at least now you don't have to worry about getting rid of his stuff." She grimaced as she listened to her own halting, rudimentary Korean, her attempts to sound lighthearted.

Ice cubes clinked in the background. Her mother, who never used to have more than a glass of wine at Christmastime, was drinking now.

"I'm just glad your grandparents aren't alive to see this. I could die of shame." Her voice sounded thin and raw with weeping.

Mia felt a thrum of anxiety in her throat, which she tried to swallow. "I'm sorry, Umma," she said, the familiar words by now a well-worn refrain. She was always apologizing to her mother for her father's mistakes. "It's late. I'll call you tomorrow, okay?"

"Call him, Mia," her mother said. "He'll listen to you. He respects you. He never respected me."

Mia's feet ached. She took another drag of her cigarette, holding the hot brick of the phone away from her ear, before promising her mother that she would. Mia and her father hadn't spoken in over three years, not since she and Peter had gotten married, and she wasn't even sure if the number she had for him still worked. But she would find a way. She always did when it came to her mother, who had only grown more fragile and needy over the years. Whether it was tracking down obscure herbal supplements on the internet that her mother swore would help with her chronic muscle aches (she refused to go to any of the specialists Mia found), or dropping off groceries on days when, convinced the neighbors were spying on her, she didn't want to leave the house, Mia had always done whatever it took to try to appease her mother without ever actually engaging with her and her endless list of worries and grievances.

After she hung up, Mia stubbed her cigarette out and took a deep breath. She turned the dishwasher on and then washed the good wineglasses, which were so large they reminded her of small fish bowls, by hand. The glasses glinted in the dim light of the kitchen, like polished molars. They had been a wedding present from Peter's parents, Jeanine and George.

Unlike their gangly son, Jeanine and George Fisher were small, compact people. They owned monogrammed towels, a dog named Ginger, a sailboat named *The Halcyon,* and a vacation home in Cape Cod that they always insisted she and Peter take advantage of. They reminded her of salt and pepper shakers, with Jeanine's white bob and George's full head of dark-gray hair.

"What's it like having parents who actually like each other?" Mia had said to Peter on the drive back after the first time she met them.

He looked at her as though he had never even considered an alternative. "I guess they're just a happy pairing," Peter said, reaching over and squeezing her hand. "Like us." She smiled back at him, telling herself how fortunate she was to be with someone so stable, so adept at being content.

Peter was tall and narrow, but he gave an impression of solidity. It was part of what had drawn her to him, the day they met at a mutual friend's thirtieth-birthday party. Mia hadn't known anyone else at the party, and neither had Peter, and so the two of them had made small talk by the coat closet until someone suggested that Peter get her number. He called her the very next day, which she had liked. Right away, things had felt intentional with Peter, serious in a way that was exciting.

Peter reminded her a little of the spacious, straightforwardly elegant Massachusetts house he had grown up in, with its tall windows, clapboard shutters, and the inviting porch that wrapped around the front like a friendly smile. She could imagine the house continuing to stand for centuries, and people who looked like Jeanine and George and Peter continuing to live in it for generations to come. But even now, three years into her marriage, she still couldn't imagine anyone who looked like her ever living there.

She drained the sink and left the wineglasses upside down to dry in the dish rack. She caught her own reflection in the window over the sink and dabbed at a wine stain on the corner of her mouth. It was almost the same shade as her new maroon lipstick, which had feathered past the edges of her lips over the course of the evening.

She considered stepping outside, standing in the dewy grass to try to catch a glimpse of the stars, which still took her by surprise on clear nights. When they first moved to this rural college town, she often stayed up late to look at them, and Peter would sometimes join her, though he didn't care much for stars. "I'm a mathematician, not a physicist," he would say when she teased him about having no soul. She would point out constellations and he would play along patiently, until he pointed out that it was getting cold and it was time to go in. Peter, always so logical.

The head of the math department, Charlie Webb, had come on to her earlier during the party, leaning in a little too close when they hugged at the door. He had greeted Peter with a hearty handshake and clapped him on the back. When she put her hand out to shake his, he had clasped it and leaned in to kiss her on the cheek, close to her right ear. She caught the scent of his cologne, something leathery and expensive, and underneath it, the smell of the mothballs his wife probably used to store his sweaters and suits.

Later, he caught up with her in the kitchen when she was cutting fruit and cheese to take out to the guests. Peter was in the living room, regaling their guests with an anecdote from his undergraduate years at MIT that she had already heard several times.

"You look like a Vermeer standing there in that light," Charlie said. "May I have a piece of fruit?"

She resisted the urge to correct him, to say that Vermeer had only ever depicted scenes in natural lighting. She remembered Peter telling her that Charlie, despite rumors of his impending retirement, was still held in high esteem at the college. Back in the seventies, he had proved some important imaginary theorem on complex numbers. Or was it a complex theorem on imaginary numbers?

She offered him a slice of the green apple she was cutting, which he accepted.

"And what do you do, my dear? Peter says you're dabbling in art history."

"I'm just finishing my master's, actually. I'm working on my thesis at the moment."

"How wonderful. I'm a bit of an art fiend myself," Charlie said. "Verna and I must have you both over for dinner soon."

"That would be great," Mia said with what she hoped was a firm, professional smile. The smile of a woman who knew she belonged, a woman who was not to be tampered or trifled with.

"Peter's a lucky man," Charlie said, biting down on the apple slice. Bits of apple flesh sprayed from his mouth as he spoke. "Lovely wife, and smart too. You remind me of an old girlfriend of mine. Keiko was her name. She made the most excellent sushi."

Mia felt her smile grow brittle. "I should really finish up here and take this in," she said.

He winked. "Come by for dinner sometime. I've got a great collection of some very special Japanese woodblock prints I'd love to show you."

After the guests had gone, she had told Peter about it, while they were cleaning up. "Japanese woodblock prints, can you imagine?" she said, ready to turn the story into something they could laugh and joke about. This was usually the part of their parties she liked best, when they stayed up late with snifters of brandy and made fun of all the people they didn't like.

"I hope you said yes," said Peter. "You know he's on my tenure review committee next year."

There was a pause. "I didn't say no. I just changed the subject," she said eventually.

"Mia," said Peter. "Be reasonable. I'm not saying you have to flatter him or flirt with him. He didn't mean anything by it. That's how men of his generation are. I'm just saying, he's an old goat, but he's still an important old goat."

Mia tried to control her voice. "That imaginary theorem he figured out must have been pretty special. Funny, your line of work. You're all always trying to prove things that are imaginary or unreal."

"Nothing funny about it," Peter said. His eyes were shining from the wine, and he sounded quarrelsome. "Math is the cornerstone of all the world's disciplines."

She put down the glass she was holding, out of a sudden fear that she would throw it at something. "Save it for your tenure review," she said.

Peter finished rinsing the plate he had been washing and left the kitchen, leaving the rest of the unwashed cups and plates for her to do. Ten minutes later, she could hear him snoring. No matter how stressed he was about departmental politics or how bad their fights were, Peter never had any trouble falling asleep. It infuriated her.

Mia shook her head, as if shaking off thoughts of Peter's irritating qualities, and glanced at the clock over the window. It was now 1:30 a.m. Mia considered calling her father's office number. Obviously, he would not be there at this time of night, but she could still call and leave a vitriolic or plaintive voicemail. Either way, the prospect of talking to her father would weigh on her mind until Monday morning.

She did not like to think of it, but she supposed that if he had finally moved out, it was time to face facts: her father, at the age of sixty-five, after nearly four decades of marriage, had left her mother. Mia found, with a sharp sense of guilt, that she could not really blame him. Her mother, who had always been what some might consider a difficult woman, could be bitter, even nasty, toward her father. Mia had not bothered to wonder why this was until she had gotten married herself and learned what it meant to be a wife.

She knew nothing of her father's new girlfriend, only that she was a former graduate student of his that he had begun seeing around the time she and Peter got married. So far she had resisted the urge to google her, but she could not be much older than Mia herself. It was part of the reason she and her father no longer spoke. It disgusted her, how disappointing and predictable her father had turned out to be.

Mia thought about the many faculty dinner parties her mother had hosted over the years, starting from when Mia was a child. All the chopping, mincing, roasting, basting, mixing, and baking she must have done.

In Mia's childhood memories, her mother consisted of two different women. One version of her mother sweated over the kitchen stove for hours, agonized over complicated French recipes, and practiced making small talk in English with Mia.

"How are you liking this weather?" Mia would say in English, giggling at what she thought was just a game.

"It's too cold. I hate it here in the winter," her mother said.

"You can't say that to people, Umma. They'll be offended."

"Ask me something else, then."

The second version of her mother, the one Mia liked better, wore silk blouses and pearly gray eye shadow, laughed politely at compliments about her food. This mother worked furiously on her thesis at night, long after everyone else had gone to bed, determined to finish her PhD and become a professor of economics herself, like Mia's father. Her father's colleagues used to ask her mother about her progress, offering to take a look at her research. But by the time Mia entered middle school, the thesis had been abandoned and was no longer brought up in conversation.

And now, thirty-eight years after her parents met as skinny graduate students and married in Seoul, before moving to a small town in Indiana (the university there having been the only place where they had both been accepted), her father had left. It was a betrayal so deep and unthinkable for Mia that she could barely comprehend it. It was almost easier to imagine that her father, who, until then, had been a solid, immovable fact of her life, had turned into a fish or a bird.

Mia turned off the kitchen light. She slipped off her tights and wadded them up in one hand as she walked to the bathroom down the hall from their bedroom, treading lightly so Peter wouldn't wake up. She brushed her teeth (making sure not to brush too hard, as her dentist had warned her not to), and stared at herself in the mirror, studying the slight bags under her eyes.

Tomorrow, she thought to herself, she and Peter would talk more about the party, and about his plans for impressing the tenure review committee, and she would nod and agree and make suggestions, because she loved him. He would do the same for her, wouldn't he? They were a happy pairing.

She would not bring up Charlie Webb or his Japanese woodblock prints again. The old goat, Peter had called him, not without affection. Within a year, he would not remember this part of the party, and she would do her best to forget it as well.

And then, once their lives slowed down and it was summer again, she would apply for jobs outside of the college, so she wouldn't have to stay in the development department, placing phone calls to alumni and crafting pithy one-liners for their email newsletter until she wanted to staple her fingers together out of boredom. She would finish her thesis and send it off to her adviser, back in New York, and then she would finally be able to tell the other faculty members and their wives that she had a master's degree in art history. She would figure out what exactly she wanted to do with the degree later.

There would even be children, at some point. Peter was ambivalent about children. But Mia thought he would probably be a good father, in the same way he was a good husband—kind, loving, and forgetful enough to believe the best of everyone.

She would call her mother tomorrow and ask her to come stay with them for a week, she decided. She would not call her father, but she would tell her mother that she had, and that no one had picked up. She would try her best to comfort her mother, to listen to her.

After spitting out the toothpaste and washing her face, Mia crept into their bedroom, where she could hear the deep, even rumbles of Peter's snores. She placed the lighter and the crumpled carton of cigarettes back into her underwear drawer, beneath the piles of lacy lingerie she never wore. It wasn't that she was trying to hide her cigarettes from Peter, not exactly. But it was nice to keep some things for herself, to have a small secret.

She plugged Peter's phone in to charge overnight, made sure to take his glasses off, and crawled into bed next to him.

The radiators in their bedroom clanked and hissed. She was too warm.

Mia closed her eyes and found herself thinking of stars again. She loved how vast and unknowable the night sky was. The sheer volume of all those stars and planetary bodies that she couldn't see but knew were there made her feel the imaginary as a possibility in her body. She found comfort in the idea that the stars existed without her, that they did not need her to notice them.

Still sleeping, Peter curled himself around her, his long hot body like a comma. In sleep his body was a furnace. Mia took slow breaths, telling herself that she was lucky, lucky to have a husband who was so loving, who had plans for their future, who was always so sure of the world and his place in it. And wasn't that what she'd always wanted, and didn't he provide that for her, a kind of certainty that she was always searching for herself?

But she thought about the cold night air, the light of the stars, and as she drifted off into an uneasy sleep, she remembered that the night held far more than what she could see with her eyes alone.

Rabbit Heart

When I am eight years old, I am a girl who would rather hide than seek, a girl who fears bullies and teachers and loud noises and speaking in public and God. I am overweight for my age group, friendless, and known for thick glasses and dark overalls, which I wear because my mother is exasperated with my clumsiness and tendency toward spillage.

But when my mother takes me to Seoul to meet my grandmother for the first time, my grandmother tells me that I am beautiful, and for a whole summer, I am. My grandmother combs my hair and braids it across the top of my head like a crown, marveling at its strength and sheen. She clucks over my glasses, at how they are almost as thick as hers, and she tells me that I have an American nose, which she says I should be proud of. She has made me dresses that do not fit, but she just laughs and lets out the seams so that they do, and I am suddenly pretty in yellow, pink, green. My mother says to Grandmother that she will spoil me, and Grandmother tells her to hush.

I twirl in the dresses for hours in Grandmother's backyard,

among the vegetables and the little white butterflies that dance from row to row. When I get dizzy, I help her pick perilla leaves, which she will wash and marinate in soy sauce, vinegar, and slivers of garlic later for dinner. "Your mother loved these when she was your age," she says. The three of us eat them under the flickering fluorescent light of her kitchen, which always smells of sesame oil and red peppers.

A cicada finds its way inside the house one evening, a wet slick of terror with too many legs and orange eyes, and my mother and I scream and scream while Grandmother chuckles. Finally, she traps it in a jar and takes it outside, where it sits, stunned, on the grass, until she shoos it away.

"You have the heart of a rabbit," she says when I tell her my fears, numbering them like my favorite songs. She tells me stories of timid rabbits who have outsmarted tigers, rabbits who have dared to visit the underwater kingdom of the Dragon King and tricked sea turtles into bringing them back to shore safely. The lesson here, she tells me, is that fear shouldn't stop you from being brave. As the summer ripens, she tells me more stories, about a snail who fell in love with a man and became a woman, a little girl who became the moon, the bear who became human after spending one hundred days in darkness eating only mugwort and garlic, and female fox demons whose heavy skirts hide their nine tails.

The air is wet and heavy in Seoul, and Grandmother's house does not have air-conditioning. I wake from nightmares in which my lungs fill with seawater, where my classmates watch me drown in a glass tank and say nothing, their blue eyes as flat as stones. On our seventh night in Seoul, when I wake up crying, Grandmother takes me to the kitchen, where she spoons strawberry ice cream into glass bowls for us while my mother sleeps, exhausted from the heat. The ice cream melts and drips down my pajama shirt a little, but, unlike my mother, my grandmother doesn't mind my mess.

When the ice cream is finished, she slices bright persimmons for us, the fleshy segments unfolding like thick petals across her cutting board. We eat them in the backyard, listening to the cicadas buzz while Grandmother points out the pale-yellow disk of the moon and shows me its grooves and shadows, which she tells me make up the silhouette of a rabbit pounding a mortar and pestle. I like the idea of a rabbit inside the moon, a small friend made of shadows and light to watch over me as I sleep.

When the summer is over, Grandmother sends me back with a sweater she knit herself, a sweater as soft as cloud-floss and as pink as strawberry ice cream. I wear it on the plane and fall asleep, and for once I do not dream that we are falling out of the sky.

Grandmother becomes a voice on the phone. "Please be healthy and live a long time," I learn to say in Korean.

"I'll try," she always says.

"When are you coming to see us?" I say, and she tells me, "Soon."

But as the years pass, Grandmother's voice on the phone fades and becomes a dry flicker of itself, and I begin to forget my halting Korean; the words of my childhood vanish as quietly as melting snow.

I grow older, taller, afraid in new ways. My fear crystallizes inside me, becoming jagged. I learn to shout back at my teachers and bullies. I am often caught fighting the other girls after school and am frequently in detention. My glasses break during one of these fights, and my mother is furious with me. We raise our voices, and the house shakes with our mutual disappointment and anger. Afterward, when I wash the tears off my face and look in the mirror, I see another girl inside me, a blurred girl filled with smoky rage.

When I am thirteen, I come home from school to find my mother sobbing in the kitchen, the phone hanging off the hook. A blood vessel migrating from one hemisphere of Grandmother's brain to the other has burst. Plane tickets are bought, bags are packed.

In the hospital, Grandmother, dressed in a patterned gown, stares at nothing, her eyes empty. The nurses tell us that she cannot hear, speak, or think, but I know she is pretending, playing a joke on all of us. The food in the hospital—gluey rice and boiled vegetables—is blanched of flavor. I tell Grandmother about it, whispering to her that the food here is terrible and that she should really wake up and tell them what's what. The machines beep in response, an electric pulse that I wonder if she can hear in her dreams.

It is our third evening in the hospital when the doctors tell us that it is time to make a decision, and my mother has to leave the room. I hear her sneakers squeak up and down the shining hallways as she cries. I reach under the covers to grab Grandmother's hand and ask her if she'd like to come home with us, fly over the ocean and around the world. "You can stay in my room," I tell her. "I can teach you English. You don't have to be alone here anymore."

Her eyes open and she turns to look at me. "Let's get out of here," she says, awake.

I help her put her shoes on and change out of her paper gown. I look away respectfully when she steps into her flowered housedress. We climb out the hospital window, shimmy down with the help of sheets knotted together, and run down the street to a nearby city park, her IV pole clattering along next to us. She is faster than I am. I imagine the look on my mother's face when she comes back to the hospital room to find the bed empty and her mother and daughter gone.

"I've always wanted to do this," Grandmother says, before detaching the IV drip neatly from her arm and rolling down a hill. Blades of grass cling to our legs, and her gown blooms with grass stains. We wait for someone to come looking for us, to shout after us and tell us that we are not allowed to be out here, but no one does. She steals a bicycle, picking the lock with a bobby pin that I loosen from my hair and hand to her as though we've done this dozens of times, and I jog up and down the sidewalk next to her as she wobbles down the street. We pick wildflowers and hand them to strangers, who smile at us. I find dandelions gone to seed for my mother, who loves their gauzy architecture.

We walk past an ice-cream shop, and I buy us two cones of strawberry. The pink sweetness drips down our wrists as we enjoy the cool night breeze. Above us, a rabbit moon rises, green and gold.

"We should be going in now," she says. "Your mother will worry."

"She always worries," I say. "I want to stay here with you."

"She worries for you," she says. "That's her job." She finishes the rest of her ice cream, crunching the cone thoughtfully.

We walk back to the hospital. She hums a song she used to sing to me on the nights I couldn't fall asleep that summer in Seoul. I don't know the words anymore, but I remember it's about a baby falling asleep alone while its mother goes to look for oysters along the beach.

I am already counting all the things about Grandmother that I will miss. Her scratchy singing voice, her cackle, the wrinkles around her eyes that make her look as though she is smiling even when she isn't, the way she smells of mothballs and sesame oil and tiger balm.

"Take care of your mother," she says, turning toward me at the entrance of the hospital.

"Don't go," I say, my mouth sour and prickly with loss.

She wraps me in her arms, and I breathe her in, one last time. She says my name, and then she vanishes completely, turning into gold crossbars of light. I walk in alone, with a fistful of dandelions. Their snowy heads nod gently as I look for my mother in the long white hallways of the hospital, to tell her that Grandmother is gone.

Presence

After Leo left, I had trouble keeping track of myself.

I had just moved into a new apartment, and I felt like I was existing in an endless twilight. I would drift off for a nap in the living room, only to find myself standing in the kitchen, washing a dish I didn't remember using. Or I would leave a cut of meat to defrost in my shining, empty refrigerator and forget it was there for days, until the sour smell of old blood dripping into the crisper reached my nose. I lay on my couch and watched car headlights and long shadows chase one another across my ceiling as the hours went by, listening to Billie Holiday and sipping whiskey. Leo had loved Billie Holiday, owned every album she'd ever made on vinyl. I wondered where all those records were now, if they were collecting dust in storage somewhere, or if they were still nestled in the built-in bookshelves in our old apartment.

The money from my divorce settlement would last me for a while, but not forever, and although I knew this, had tallied up the remaining numbers in my accounts to determine how long I'd be able to go without seeking new employment, I couldn't bring myself to begin the process of starting afresh. Despite the genericness of my name, Amy Hwang, even the most negligent recruiter or hiring manager could find out everything they needed to know about my connections to Gnoss and its founder with even a cursory Google search.

I stared into the abyss of my past accomplishments, listed row by row on a CV that I had once been so pleased about, so proud of compiling, like a house I had laid brick by brick. Now I felt as though I was staring out through the bars of a locked window in that same house, imprisoned by the vestiges of a life that would never be mine again.

I ignored all incoming calls, except for Lila's. Lila and I were roommates throughout most of college, and though we were never very close, we had remained in each other's lives long after our relationships with our other friends had faded. We were different enough that we never felt threatened by each other's news or achievements. We were barely a year out of college when she showed up to one of our infrequent drinks dates with a diamond on her finger and photos on her phone of a clean-cut, handsome man with family money and a history of successful investments. Her husband bought her a boutique, where she sold designer clothing for children in soft colors like oatmeal, blush, and buttercup. In other words, Lila had a lot of time on her hands, and she prided herself on knowing just how to use that time. She knew the perfect place for everything, from sunrise yoga to natural wines, and she often posted about all her experiences on the internet. She was a member of Yelp Elite, a superuser whose enthusiastic or negative review of a restaurant, riddled with exclamation points and emojis and cross-posted to her Instagram, could be significant for a new business.

So when Lila told me about a spa she knew of and offered me her upcoming reservation there, I thought, *Why not?* Leo used to say that I never knew when to take a break, that this was one of the things we had in common, and it's true—I always felt guilty whenever we took vacations away from the company, and I have never been a person who enjoys relaxation rituals. But I had also thought I was not the kind of woman who would find herself newly divorced at the age of thirty-six, blocking all unknown numbers and deleting all of her social-media profiles to avoid reporters' insistent and aggressive messages, and ordering everything online so she wouldn't run into anyone she knew on the street. So many unprecedented things had already happened to me; I figured, what was one more?

"The location alone is so worth it," Lila said. "It's far away from everything, and there's hardly even phone service out there. It's the perfect place to rest and recharge."

Lila was the first person I called when the news about Gnoss came out—the accusations of falsified lab results, the lawsuits. She flew out to New York City from LA and rubbed my back while I sat numbly in our living room, the room I had so proudly and lovingly decorated. "It's not your fault, Amy," she kept repeating soothingly. "You didn't know."

The drive to the spa would take me about four hours, so I left the city hours before sunrise, when the traffic was sparse and the sky was still dark. I stopped for coffee and gas at a station along the thruway. I considered keeping my sunglasses on when I entered the convenience store, but decided that I would probably not be recognized up here. The clerk barely looked up from her phone to give me my change, and I relaxed, the coins warm in the palm of my hand. Leo never carried cash, so I was always the one who had to bring it in case we went to a place that didn't take cards.

He hated bothering with currency, but I liked having money in my hands, the rustle of green bills and the weight of metal coins in my wallet. We used to joke that it was the immigrant in me, even though I was technically the child of immigrants.

When I got back into the car, the presence was there, in the passenger seat. It must have crept in sometime during the drive up, or while I was in the gas station. I could practically taste it behind my teeth. It watched me as I took the first few scalding sips of gas-station coffee, made no better by the addition of slightly sour milk. My head began to ache, the way it usually did around the presence.

There was no use in trying to avoid it. "Hello, old friend," I said. It did not respond. It never did, no matter how many times I addressed it or implored.

I tried to settle my nerves by fiddling with the radio and landed on a country station. I turned it up, a familiar electricity rushing through me when I realized it was a song I had loved once, long before I'd ever met Leo. I sang along to the radio, and we continued up the thruway without stopping along the way. The radio continued playing ancient hit after ancient hit as I rolled the windows down, letting the wind whip my hair into a greasy frenzy. I caught my reflection in the rearview mirror and noted idly to myself that I was starting to go gray, lines of iron interrupting the long coils of black.

The sun rose yellow outside. I wondered what kinds of treatments the spa would offer. Despite the events of the last few months, I finally began to look forward to my stay. I managed to mostly forget that the presence was there, though I continued to feel its magnetic pull.

The air grew sharper and the trees grew taller and darker as we wended our way farther north, especially once I'd turned off the main thruway. We passed through small, sleepy towns with names like Cheshire and Hancock, towns that seemed like they hadn't changed at all in the last few decades. American flags and festive scarecrows beckoned from every porch. Soon it would be autumn, time for leaf-peeping and apple-picking. Leo and I had gone apple-picking once, not long after we'd gotten married, on a rare weekend when neither of us had to work. I was twenty-eight then, determined to live up to the role of younger, vivacious wife that I was aware had been assigned to me. We wore coordinating plaid flannel shirts and posed dutifully for photos next to the trees we picked our apples from, though more often than not we decided to go for the fruit that was already on the ground. When we got home, we found that almost all of the apples were filled with worms.

The houses grew taller and narrower when we entered Vermont. Picturesque views of peaked roofs, church steeples, and treetops began to appear outside the car. The sound of the radio grew fuzzy, and the voices faded in and out behind waves of static. I turned it off and listened to the quiet and the hiss of my tires on the tarmac as I navigated the sloped roads. I could feel the presence pulling at the edges of my consciousness again. My headache sharpened.

Leo had been my lab supervisor at Columbia when I was a PhD student. At first, I didn't notice him much beyond the functional role he played in the lab, fixated as I was then on getting ahead, ignoring the statistics about how hard it was for women to succeed in the sciences. *I am going to be the exception to every rule,* I told myself. I would graduate well within the expected time frame of seven years. I would author several papers, all of which would be published in reputable journals. I would find a tenured teaching job at a prestigious university.

Leo was much taller than he seemed when he was sitting

down, with narrow shoulders and a shock of thick graying hair. He had a loud, braying laugh that was both disconcerting and disarming, the kind of laugh that turned heads and flattered its recipient into thinking they'd said something notably witty. He gave everyone nicknames, including me, calling me "Aimless," which was his way of making a joke, because I was anything but that. Though I have never been a naturally gifted or brilliant student, I have always prided myself on my diligence and my ability to focus for long periods of time.

I was not popular in our lab, given that I seldom joined the team for after-work drinks or weekend Frisbee games. But the work (we were studying immune-system responses in mice experiencing environmental stressors) was enthralling. Once, on a slower day when I had gotten particularly in the zone, Leo had to shake me to alert me that the fire alarm was going off. We were the only ones in the lab that day. I was preparing to give one of the mice an injection of the serum we were testing them with, when I was startled by the weight of a hand on my shoulder.

"Amy! Didn't you hear the alarm?" Leo loomed above me, looking concerned and, for some reason, a little angry. I stammered out an apology, put the syringe and the quivering mouse away, and shuffled outside with him. It was just a routine fire inspection, and afterward Leo found me in the lab and apologized for startling me. "I've never seen someone with the ability to focus the way you can. It's a little scary," he said.

"Thank you?" I said.

"I mean that in a good way, mostly," he said. It wasn't until he'd walked back to his station that I realized he'd called me Amy, instead of Aimless.

A few years later, when Leo left the university to start Gnoss and asked me to join him, telling me he'd make me the head of one of its most important projects, Lila urged me to go for it. "But my degree," I said weakly. She pointed out how miserable academia made me, all my years of toiling away in the lab, applying for grants I didn't get and struggling to get my name on papers that I had coauthored with the (mostly) white men I worked with. And it was true that my heart was no longer in my work, my project having stalled for years while I remained unable to obtain the results I needed to finish. The confidence and certainty that had once fueled me, given me the kind of laser focus other people had to take drugs to obtain, was in tatters, a ragged white flag where there had once been a victory banner.

She counseled me through signing the onboarding papers and the NDA, and, once I was hired, instructed me on how to respond in a flirtatious but still-professional way to Leo's increasingly frequent and informal emails asking for status updates about my project. When he finally asked me out, she told me what to wear, how to wear it, and why I should wait to have sex with him until our third date.

It was 11:30 a.m. by the time I reached the hidden lane that supposedly led to the spa. I almost missed the gate and had to reverse the car back to it. *Welcome to Dripping Pines Spa and Sanatorium*, read a small hand-painted sign. Sanatorium? I blinked, and then the letters rearranged themselves to form *Sanctuary*. I was tired from the drive, wired from the coffee, I thought. I prepared myself to step outside of the car, to punch in the code that Lila had given me, but the gate slid open without any prompting. I guided the car in through the narrow opening and down the well-paved driveway, which was bordered by trees and white stones. It led to a small lot, where I parked. Mine was the only car there, besides a blue Honda Civic that I assumed must belong to the proprietor. "You'll love Ruth," Lila had said of her. "Make sure you request the hot-stone massage. It did wonders for my lower back."

I walked inside, where a fountain burbled in an atrium. The presence followed me, as unnervingly patient as always. An unseen diffuser emitted puffs of orange fragrance into the air. "Hello?" I called. Low tones and chants played softly in the background.

"You're early," said the woman behind the desk. I had expected a willowy white blonde wearing prayer beads and a caftan, but this woman wore a blazer over a turtleneck, and she was tan, with silvery hair cut into a neat bob, and she was Asian. I had not expected to see another Asian person this far up north. She stared at me over her rimless glasses for a beat too long, and I was wondering if she was thinking the same thing. "I can't let you in with that," she said, finally.

I felt chills rush up to the surface of my skin. No one else I'd ever met before could see the presence. I felt it pulse silently beside me.

"Please," I said. To my surprise, my eyes filled with tears. I must have been very tired from the drive. "I came all this way. I'll pay extra."

The woman studied me. "Sit down," she said, gesturing toward a rattan stool. I sat and wiped my eyes. She disappeared down a hallway and reemerged with a cup of hot tea. I let it steam my face.

"It's been with you for quite some time," she said. "I can't remove it for you, but it can be contained."

I nodded, momentarily blind from the steam. My entire body felt sore. All I wanted was to rest, to lie down, to let the fatigue of the last few months overtake me. I took a sip of the tea. It tasted like ginger and tree bark.

"You'll have to keep this on during your time here," she said. She slipped a wooden cuff around my right wrist. It was made of a plain, polished dark wood. "That should help somewhat," she said. "Rowan is good for protection. I'll show you to your room now."

"Thank you," I said to her back as I followed her down the halls. She did not reply or turn around. Behind me, I felt the presence trailing me, a discreet distance away.

Leo had started Gnoss to address the problem of memories that no longer needed to be retained. "The brain is simply a hard drive," he was always saying. "We do periodic data dumps on our personal devices to keep them running smoothly, so why not our minds? Why can't we simply upload the memories we no longer need?" His model was simple—monthly memory data-collection scans, which could be performed at any Gnoss facility. After anywhere from five to ten scan sessions (depending on the number of memories a client had developed over the course of their lifetime), Gnoss would build the client a mind map, called a Chartis, of their own memories that they could then manipulate, categorize, and organize, choosing which memories to retain and which to upload to their own personal, private memory clouds. According to Leo, uploading traumatic, difficult, or simply unnecessary memories would alleviate day-to-day stress levels, improve relationships with others, and combat trauma-induced insomnia and other psychosomatic disorders, thereby allowing clients to take back control of their lives. And though reversing the process was more difficult than undergoing it, it was doable, in case the user wanted to recover any of the memories that they had previously uploaded.

I became part of a new initiative that was testing Gnoss's latest innovation, Neolaia. Unlike the original Chartis process, which could take up to eight months depending on the number of scans that were deemed necessary, Neolaia was a shortcut—a flat metal disk the size of a dime that, when adhered to the skin, could absorb enough data overnight to create a simple mind map that the user could access via the Gnoss app. With Neolaia, Chartis creation now took only a matter of hours, and even though the resulting mind map wasn't as complex or sophisticated as the map developed by the usual Gnoss scans, now almost anyone with a WiFi connection could take advantage of the technology to organize and optimize their memories, up to a point. It also meant, thanks to the lower production costs of the device, that we could now offer Gnoss's services at a significantly lower price point, and eventually phase out the original Chartis process.

Leo's hope was that Gnoss's treatments would also, over time, lead to decreases in more inscrutable psychiatric disorders, such as Alzheimer's and dementia. He had lost his father to Alzheimer's when the man was only fifty-five, a fact that I knew haunted him, especially as his own age crept upward. My mother had also had the disease, which was part of the reason we had connected in the first place, and why he had hired me. "You have a personal connection to this," he told me over our first lunch meeting. "I need top-notch people, but also people who get it. People whose actual lives have been destroyed by this." He spoke of Alzheimer's sometimes as though it were a human foe, an archenemy in need of vanquishing.

When I was in high school, my mother began roaming around the neighborhood on her own, sometimes without shoes, and often without a clear explanation for what she had been doing or looking for. She was fine in the mornings—calm, sweet-tempered even—but as night fell she would become angry with me, sometimes accusing me of lying to her over trivial things, like where I'd put the salt. Her condition rapidly worsened when I was in college. With my father at work, she was left largely alone during the day. I didn't tell any of my friends, even Lila, about it, about how my father had to lock my mother in their bedroom at night, or how she would forget his face and scream when he approached her. It was easier to bear that way. I continued to go to class and excel in my studies, but between the hours of midnight and 7:00 a.m., I was completely unable to sleep. If I did fall asleep, which I seldom did, I usually woke up an hour or so later and lay awake, paralyzed by anxiety, until the morning light streamed through my curtains.

My mother finally died when I was in my twenties, and afterward, my father and I, who had never been very close, drifted further apart. He moved back to Korea, and our messages to each other grew increasingly infrequent, until they took on the tone of communications between polite, apologetic acquaintances. He remarried when I was twenty-five. "I'm sorry not to have told you sooner. I know you were probably busy with work," he said when he wrote with the news. He sent me photos of my half-sisters sometimes, two little girls who looked nothing like me.

Not long after I joined Gnoss, I began the Chartis process myself. I decided to upload those core memories of my mother and her decline to my cloud, so that, while I could remember the basic facts and chronology of what had happened to her, I was no longer troubled by the sense memories that had plagued me before, like the stale smell of her nursing facility; the way her terrified and rageful eyes followed me around the room whenever I came to visit; or the exact tone and timbre of her voice when she confused me with someone else and accused me of stealing from her. I filed each of the memories away, labeled them, and then thought no more of them.

Afterward, I slept soundly for the first time in years. My skin cleared and my digestion improved, as did my overall sense of well-being. I took deeper breaths, became more generous with myself and my colleagues and friends. I no longer felt racked by guilt and grief. Gone were my sleepless nights, the nightmares, the grinding of teeth that made my dentist warn me that I'd be left with nothing but a mouthful of dust by the age of fifty if I didn't change my lifestyle.

It was then that the presence first arrived. I woke one night to find it sitting on my bed, regarding me quietly. *I've been working too hard,* I told myself, *I'm seeing things.* But the next morning it was still there. And though it sometimes went away for a while, it always came back, no matter where I went or what was going on in my life. Leo never saw it, and I never pointed it out to him, afraid of what might happen, of whether he would look at me as if I were crazy. *Besides,* I told myself, *if I don't pay attention to it, it might just leave on its own.*

But as time went on, the presence grew stronger and more insistent, especially whenever I asked it to leave. I wondered if it felt it was owed something for its years of loyalty. Sometimes, it tugged at my attention like a recalcitrant dog at its leash, distracted me, made my head throb.

I tried to find out if it was an as yet unknown side effect of the Chartis process. But Gnoss had reached unicorn status three months before I joined, and demand was high across all market sectors, including among seemingly "normal" individuals, many of them high-functioning and quite successful. According to their introductory questionnaires, the typical Gnoss client hadn't experienced more than the average number of Adverse Life Experiences (or ALEs), but simply wanted to "optimize" their cognitive and memory skills by data dumping the memories they no longer needed.

Our testimonials were overwhelmingly positive. Even users with the most challenging types of ALEs—abuse and assault victims; addicts; war veterans; the recently bereaved—all of them found reprieve from the memories of their traumatic experiences via the Chartis process, and not one of them, even those who had experienced the few negative side effects like occasional nausea or sleepiness, ever reported being followed around by a shadowy presence that no one else could see.

My room at Dripping Pines was small and plainly furnished, with one bed and a desk and chair, but it was well kept and tidy. I hung the few clothes I had brought with me in the closet and sat down on the narrow bed to stare out the window, at the murmuration of green and sunlight outside. It was warm outside, but early September in the mountains of New England meant that the temperature would dip below fifty degrees in the evening. I studied the informational brochure that the woman had left behind. "Spa hours are ten a.m. to five p.m. every day," she had said. "Lunch and dinner are served at twelve p.m. and six p.m. No bathing after hours, no exceptions."

The spa setup was simple. There was a sauna, made of teak, into which steam was piped, and two pools in a large, tiled room. The first pool was heated and smelled of eucalyptus and rosemary. The second was kept cold and filled with salt water. Additional services, like massages or private soaking baths, were also available upon request. My room was stocked with fluffy white towels, a plush bathrobe, a pair of slippers, and a pair of rubber flip-flops. I was surprised by the simplicity of it all, as it did not seem like the kind of place Lila would rave about—her tastes were generally more refined—but I could tell that everything, including the bed linens, was of the highest quality.

I kept the bracelet on at all times, even bringing it into the shower with me, and I felt the presence at a remove, as though it were not allowed to come within a certain distance of me when I was wearing it.

Over the next few days, I rarely saw the woman at the front desk, and it wasn't until my third day there that I realized I didn't even know her name, if she was the Ruth that Lila had told me about. Nor had she asked for mine, not even to check what name the reservation was under.

The waters softened my skin and hair. I felt relaxed and clearheaded in a way I had not been in quite some time. At lunch, I took my simple meal of porridge, vegetables, and a boiled egg, which was always prepared in advance and left for me on a tray in the large dining area, outside. The spa was indeed a sanctuary, and some areas of the grounds were marked as being off-limits to guests because certain migratory birds liked to nest there. I knew nothing about birds, but I felt my heart lift when I began to recognize their bands and markings, and the sounds they made when they called to one another.

Lila had been right about the lack of phone service. I had just enough in the parking lot to send a text, but not enough to call anyone. At first, I considered asking the woman at the front desk if there was at least a WiFi network I could connect to, but as the days went by, I found the absence of the internet from my life a welcome change. It was a relief not to feel the need to check in with the world, not to tense up every time a name or a call flashed across my screen that could be someone asking me how I was doing, or a reporter seeking a quote.

At night, I slept soundly, so soundly that I was even starting to remember my dreams. I used to have the most vivid dreams when I was younger, so vivid that I would sometimes wake up laughing or crying, or to the sound of my own voice carrying on a conversation or arguing with a dream person. After the Chartis process, my dreams had become harder and harder to remember. I had started trying to track them in a journal, after a brief fit of attempting to learn about dream analysis and interpretation, though I rarely remembered anything significant enough to write down.

But at the spa, I found myself falling asleep earlier and earlier each night, satisfied by the simple but hearty food and worn out from another day of bathing and sweating and walking up and down the gently sloping hills of the spa's grounds. And I dreamt about fantastical situations, in colors so bright that when I woke up I found myself wondering if I was still sleeping and had passed into another dream, because the real world seemed almost unrecognizable for the first few seconds.

On my third night at the spa, I dreamt that I lived in a house that stood on two scaly legs, like a dinosaur. Inside, my bed was lofted, an airy nest under which I cooked and washed and ate. There, I found a cat, curled up in a corner. She was a beauty, with dark-gray fur and bright-blue eyes. She purred at me and swished her long tail. When I returned from fetching her a bowl of milk, she was gone. In her place was a small orange kitten, with tiny, tufted ears like a bobcat's. He let me trail my fingers over his fur and pet him, rubbing him under the chin and behind his ears. He curled himself around my ankles like a sentient ribbon and followed me as I tidied up, underneath the great lofted bed. When I turned around, he had vanished, and there was instead a large white cat with a round, squashed face, whose flat yellow eyes regarded me with dull disdain. *Hello there,* I said, and I offered him my hand to sniff. Instead, he unhinged his jaw and encaged my hand in his cavernous mouth. I could feel his small but pointed teeth digging into my flesh. I wondered if I would lose a finger. I had to pry his jaws off my wrist, as though he were an alligator and not a cat.

In the morning, my whole body was tense and sore, as though I really had been wrestling with a cat. I decided to book a massage. I needed to feel human fingers prodding and digging into my flesh, to rearrange and pummel my body.

I showed up at the front desk at the appointed time, to find the woman who had greeted me on the first day there. "Our usual masseuse is out of town," she said. "I'll be taking care of you." She began walking down a corridor to the left of the entrance that I hadn't noticed before. She inquired after my health, asking me how I had been sleeping lately.

"Very well, though I keep having the strangest dreams. And today I woke up feeling as though I'd been walking for miles."

"Many of our clients report the same thing during their first few nights here. Our spa is quite haunted, you know." She said this very casually, as though she were telling me about some inclement weather we were due to experience later that week. "You didn't happen to dream about cats, did you?"

I almost stopped in my tracks. "I did, as a matter of fact."

"They belonged to the previous owner," she said. "They show up in my dreams, too. They died in the fire."

"There was a fire?" I asked. Lila had said nothing about this in her descriptions of the spa. I stared at the woman's taut back as she continued walking down the hallway. She didn't respond.

The massage room was dimly lit; the shades were drawn. A diffuser in the corner piped out lavender-scented clouds, which made me feel drowsy. She handed me a plush white towel and a yellow robe. "You'll need to take off the bracelet, too," she said. "I'll give you a few minutes to get settled."

The door closed, and I undressed, slipping out of my clothes, and settled myself on the massage table. I hesitated before removing the bracelet, and when I did, I could feel, with a disorienting whoosh, the presence slide into the room with me, its familiar heaviness making it a bit harder than usual to breathe.

"So it's still with you," she said when she returned.

I felt cold pinpricks run up and down my exposed spine. "How is it that you can see it?" I asked. "No one else has ever been able to."

The lights dimmed further, and the scents of ginger and jasmine filled the air. She was dripping oil onto her palms. "Perhaps they weren't looking closely enough," she said.

Her hands were strong, her fingers supple. She began with my head, massaging my scalp, before moving down my neck to rub the tendons and cords there. As her hands traveled across my shoulder blades and down my back, a deep well of feeling began to open up inside me. The heat emanating from her hands felt almost unbearable. I felt as though I would start to shake or cry. I took a deep breath and waited for the well to close back up.

Gnoss went public the same year that Neolaia became available in the North American, European, and Asian markets. Leo was ecstatic. For once, he seemed happy with what he had accomplished, instead of brooding on what could have gone better or what was next. And although it wasn't like I hadn't been expecting our lives to change, it still took me by surprise, the influx of wealth and exposure Gnoss's success brought us. We moved into a new apartment, bought vacation homes, pieds-à-terre. Leo, never one for flash, or so I'd thought, got a few luxury cars. We went for joyrides together in them, the wind streaming in through the open roof as we held hands and blasted his favorites—the Talking Heads, the Pixies, the Doors. By then, I knew all the words to the songs he'd grown up listening to and I hadn't.

He appeared regularly on the covers of magazines and the front pages of national newspapers, and I was interviewed for women's glossies and talk shows. I was given a stylist, for public appearances. I found the attention uncomfortable at first, but I grew used to it, and to all the attendant perks and benefits.

Privately, I tried not to think about what the larger implications of Gnoss's developments might be, what could happen to a society in which memories were no longer something you inevitably had to live with until they faded away or were replaced by others. I ignored the usual doomsdayers, the op-eds and forecasters who warned of dire times, of loosening moral standards and the potential for dictators, predators, and abusers to take advantage of the tech to further subjugate their victims or inoculate them from the consequences of what had been done to them. *We're helping people,* I thought. I told myself that Leo was a visionary, that Gnoss was, in fact, changing the world in a way that so many tech and biotech companies promised to but never could.

"Extraordinary people aren't bound by ordinary rules," Leo liked to say. I never asked if he thought I was extraordinary, because I didn't think I had to. After all, he had asked me, of all of us at Columbia, to go with him. With Leo, I never had to worry that he would think less of me for putting my work and ambitions ahead of other matters. Unlike other men I'd dated in the past, he didn't balk at my insistence that I didn't want children and never would, as he felt similarly. Gnoss, what he was building there—that was our baby, our shared vision.

When the news about the Chartis process and its drawbacks started breaking, I tuned out, refusing to look at the reports and even ignoring company emails, worded in polite, smooth tones, about what was going on, and reminding employees that they were bound by company policy to avoid speaking to the media. But it was hard to avoid the stories, the footage, the countless interviews. One woman, a childhood cult victim who had used Neolaia to dispense with her most difficult memories of the abuse she had suffered during her family's time in the sect, was interviewed in a nightly news segment. She could barely string together her sentences, and had to be reminded several times of who she was. Her face was blurred out, for privacy, and the network referred to her as Cynthia.

"What would you say," the host said, leaning forward sympathetically in his chair and narrowing his eyes, "is the most debilitating side effect?"

Cynthia began to cry. "I can't remember anything. Anything at all." The camera panned away from the blur of her face over to the host, who pursed his lips and reached across the space between them to hold her hand.

"You're somewhere far away," the woman said.

"I'm sorry," I said.

"I'm going to ask you to turn over now," she said. I obeyed. I closed my eyes as her hands traveled down my legs, handling my calf muscles with strength and tenderness. I realized, with a small shudder of sadness, that I couldn't remember the last time I'd been touched.

"So how long has it been with you?" she asked. It took me a moment to understand what she meant by "it." I tried to tamp down my awareness of the presence. I could feel it—not in the room with us, but on the outer margins of my consciousness—watching and waiting.

"About five years," I said.

"And have you ever seen anyone about it?" she asked.

"To be honest, it's not something I felt I could ever explain to anyone," I said.

"Maybe you should have tried," she said. I felt annoyed at the cool remove in her tone, the impression she gave that it was somehow my fault that I had been dogged by the presence for so long.

We didn't speak for the rest of the session. My breath slowed again as I relaxed back into the massage. I felt like I was floating above my own body, watching it be handled and squeezed and kneaded like dough. The rope of tension that banded my muscles loosened, as though she were undoing its knots.

As a child, I was plagued by indigestion, and my mother would often massage my hands, pinching what she told me were pressure points that would help with the sharp, stabbing pains in my stomach. When I complained that it hurt, she would shush me. "Pain isn't always bad," she said. "It's there because it wants to tell us something."

What we didn't think to take into account: Neolaia was perhaps making the Chartis process too easy.

It wasn't immediately apparent that something was wrong, in our initial trials. Some of our subjects did experience side effects like mild disorientation and vertigo—nothing to be alarmed about. I took notes, ran trial after trial, wrote up reports.

"We have full confidence in Neolaia's potential to further the overall goals of Gnoss's mission," I wrote in my final report. "Chartis production time has been significantly decreased throughout our trials, and while data integrity is always a concern when it comes to scalable tech, our main objectives, to increase accessibility and intelligibility, have been achieved. We have no reason to believe that further beta tests are needed at this time, and are excited to recommend Neolaia production be ramped up to full capacity."

What I didn't tell Leo was that the first time I'd received access to my own Chartis, I was immediately hooked by the simplicity and beauty of it. I tried, somewhat successfully, to ignore the urge to continue purging my memories, to discard everything I no longer needed. I also ignored reports from my own team about how some of our subjects experienced a significant downturn in their mental and emotional well-being in the months after undergoing the Chartis process via Neolaia. I told them that their data were insubstantial and that they had better run the numbers again to come up with better ones.

"Are you sure?" Leo asked me later at home.

"Are you doubting my results?" I said. He'd assured me early on in our relationship that I'd have complete freedom in my lab and my clinical trials, that he'd never take advantage of our personal connection to weigh in on my professional findings.

"Never," he said, leaning in to kiss me. We were grilling vegetables and plant-based burgers. It was late summer. I was slicing lemons and making salad dressing. "I just want to make sure we're ready. This is a turning point for Gnoss. For us."

"I know that," I said. "And I'm telling you that Neolaia is good to go. The sooner we can roll it out the better, right?"

"Look at you," he said, amused. "Usually, you're the one telling me to slow things down, to check all the data twice."

"Maybe you're rubbing off on me," I said. I had been heading up our efforts around Neolaia for nearly three years at that point, and I was eager for it to debut on the markets, to make my mark as more than just the wife of Gnoss's founder. I knew what my peers thought of me, that I had only gotten to my position—my own credentials and years of experience had no bearing, of course—because I had been sleeping with the boss. And there it was again, that surging sense of certainty and drive, as slippery and silver as a fresh fish, almost as though it had never left me. I felt the urge to make something of myself, to prove people wrong, to achieve something again.

They say you'll never go broke underestimating people's intelligence. The same goes for their willingness to avoid feeling discomfort. When memories are the medium through which we experience most of our emotions and relive our highest and lowest moments, it makes sense that, after a while, it would become addictive to edit, delete, and manipulate them over and over again, in search of a clean slate. A place beyond pain.

Early user complaints about Neolaia were smoothed over easily enough. Minor kinks, I told myself and my team. But when a news story broke about how a prominent senator in Illinois who had lost her teenage son in a drunk-driving incident years earlier was found wandering the cornfields of her hometown, weeping and clutching his school uniform—that was the beginning of the end. The senator had been a Neolaia user, and had, in her determination to keep her grief from derailing her career, uploaded too many memories in one go. An emergency redownload of her memories was planned, but it was too late—so many of her memories had been threaded through with thoughts of her son that it became impossible to detangle them from the ones she needed in order to function normally. She ended up in a nursing home, unable to articulate her sorrow or remember her own name.

After the hearings and the consumer lawsuits, it was ruled that some users' adverse reactions to Neolaia were not due to faults with the technology, which worked as promised. Leo was allowed to stay on as CEO. The company pivoted. In the end, it was me and the rest of the high-level Neolaia team leads who took the fall. And, still, I knew I was lucky that the only fallout I really experienced, at the end of it all, was in legal fees and the dissolution of my marriage and my career.

After the massage, I felt wrung out, loose, like a newly washed garment. I thanked the woman and wobbled to my feet, wrapped myself in the complimentary robe. I imagined I would go back to my room, pass out for another night of sleep. Instead, she offered me a joint.

"Smoking after a massage is the best," she said. "It goes through the body as clean as a knife."

It turned out she was right. We sat outside, watching the last of the sunlight fade from the purple-edged mountains, and passed the joint between us. The air was thick with the smell of chamomile and weed. My limbs felt pleasantly heavy.

"It's good to remember how big the world is," the woman said. She seemed younger like this, with her glasses pushed up onto her hair and her eyes half closed in relaxation.

"How long have you been doing this?" I said.

"This?"

"Massage therapy. Running this place."

She smiled. "Too long to remember," she said. "I used to be like you. I had big plans, once. Now my days have a slower rhythm."

"But you don't know anything about me," I said, bristling slightly.

"Don't have to," she said. "Everyone who comes here is running away from something. The body reveals everything, if you know how to listen to it."

Birds called to one another as twilight fell. I wondered what story my body told. What secrets and hidden sorrows it still contained, despite my best attempts to erase them from my mind. How arrogant and foolish I had been, to think that I could outrun myself. As if on cue, my head twanged again as the presence hovered nearby.

"You've forgotten who you are," the woman said. I felt my breath catch. "That's what it wants. It's just trying to remind you. That's all."

"What about you?" I asked.

"What about me?"

"You said everyone who comes here is running away from something."

She took one last drag of the joint. The sweet-acrid smell of weed hung in the air. The setting sun illuminated her face, turning her golden.

"It's better to hold on to some things," she said enigmatically. "Besides, I'm not running anymore."

That night, the cats appeared to me again in my dreams. They wound themselves all around me, nuzzling my chest and face. The dark-gray cat sat on my chest, while the orange cat, which was now an adult, butted his head against mine. The white cat watched us impassively, switching his tail from side to side. Tongues of red flame licked the walls, but there was no heat. I passed one hand through the fire and watched as it came out unscathed. "Do you see this?" I asked the cats, marveling. They yawned, bored.

When I woke, the presence was sitting at the foot of my bed, just like it used to. I had forgotten to put the wooden bracelet on after my massage. "I'm sorry," I said. "I'm sorry I left you behind." It watched me, silently insistent. It seemed to need me to bear witness to it, acknowledge its shape and heft. I reached for it, and my hands passed through its dark, transparent membrane. I knew then what I had to do.

"Leaving already?" the woman said when I emerged from my room with my bags the next morning. "Most people tend to want to extend their reservations here."

"I should be getting back," I said. "I've been away for long enough."

"I hope you find what you're looking for," she said. She touched my arm, lightly. "There's space for you here, whenever you want to come back."

"Thank you," I said. I handed her the wooden bracelet, which she accepted with a slight nod.

She came outside to watch me leave. I waved before I pulled out of the parking lot, and she raised one hand in reply. When she turned to go back inside, I thought I could see three tails—orange, white, and gray—floating behind her in the doorway.

The ride back seemed to pass much faster than the way up had. I didn't play the radio, just rolled the windows down and let the wind sing in my ears. The narrow, winding roads soon widened into highways, and my car was joined by others, all heading south. Beside me, the presence waited, as silent and faithful as an old dog. Whenever I began to feel afraid of what lay ahead, I allowed its weight on my mind to soothe me, to bring me back to the road and the feeling of my hands around the steering wheel, guiding us home.

After Leo left me, I deleted the bulk of our later memories together. I didn't want to be reminded of what exactly we'd said to each other, how much we'd hurt each other. I didn't want to remember the look of anger and recrimination on his face as he

accused me of sabotaging his work, of hurting the company. I
didn't want to think about how he'd instructed his lawyers and
Gnoss's PR team to craft a carefully worded statement implying that the user issues lay with Neolaia and, more specifically,
with me and my failures, my negligence. I held on to just enough
about those days to stay abreast of the details, to protect myself.
But his facial expressions, the last things he ever said to me—
the shards of memory that had caused me the most pain—
I removed those exact particulars from my mind, so that when
I considered those last few weeks and months, it felt like I was
wandering around a half-built, abandoned house, with gaping
holes where there should be scaffolding, or reading a letter sent
during wartime, with several words and passages redacted by a
censor's heavy black lines.

I didn't know if I was ready to bring it all back, to inhabit once
more the dark rooms and passageways of my memories and all
they held. But it was time to stop stepping around them.

When I arrived at my building, it felt as though I'd been away for
months, rather than just under a week. I hesitated before fitting
my key into the lock, certain that I had the wrong unit, that I
had confused the one above or below mine with my own. I was
still unused to this apartment, and had almost, on the way back,
turned my car toward the home that Leo and I once shared, out
of pure instinct.

But upon entering the apartment, I felt at ease. There were
my books, my things, the few items of furniture I'd managed to
purchase in recent months, including the bed where I slept alone
each night. The presence followed me as I shut the door and
locked it. It settled throughout my apartment like a fine layer
of dust, and I realized that I hadn't had a headache at all on the
ride down.

My phone buzzed with a message from Lila. "So how was the trip? How are you feeling?" I ignored it.

I sat down at my scarred wooden desk and opened the right drawer, the one that always got stuck. The presence watched me as I felt around inside until I found what I was looking for— a dime-sized metal disk. It warmed at my touch. I placed it on my left wrist, waiting for the familiar pressure on my skin, the low hum that meant it was booting up.

I opened my computer to the Neolaia app and found the folder containing all of my data files. There it all was, in color-coded and alphabetized order—every memory I'd ever flinched away from, that I'd deemed too heavy to carry with me. I highlighted all of them and found the menu options I needed.

ARE YOU SURE YOU WANT TO REDOWNLOAD? A message asked me in flashing red letters.

I clicked YES and closed my eyes. The disk grew warmer and began whirring softly.

I sat back and waited to feel everything.

Human Hearts

Mother has always called me weak. I am too softhearted, she says, to be a real kumiho. "You must take after your father in that way, Okja," she says, teeth flashing with disdain when she sees me balk at an easy kill. She often says this—that I must take after my father—whenever she finds me lacking.

Mother often remarks on the differences between me and my twin sister, Mija. Mija's eyes were a bright gold and her fur was russet, the color of fallen leaves in autumn, whereas mine is a dull, tawny brown. Even in human form, Mija was lovely, with large eyes and thick, glossy hair that streamed down her back when it was loose.

Mija has been dead for seven days now. Mother was coming home with two ducks in her mouth for dinner when she found her, not far from the mouth of our den. "Why weren't you watching for her?" she screamed at me. The mountains echoed with her reproach, and the additional, unspoken question: Why had Mija succumbed to a shaman's poisoned snare, and not me?

Kumiho are much stronger and cleverer than humans, but

we are not immune to their wiles. The mingled smells of poison and magic that surrounded Mija's body made me feel dizzy. Mija would have smelled it, too, but she could never resist a challenge. The smell of fresh blood must have driven her beyond reason and made her decide that the tender haunch of rabbit inside the snare was worth the risk. Mija had eluded hunters' traps before, slipping past their clever nets to mouth a piece of meat delicately and steal away without getting caught. But the hexes must have weakened her body the moment the snare tightened around her paw, making her vulnerable to the poison that had been braided into the rope of the snare.

We have burned Mija's body, so that the spells that killed her will not be transferred to us. Mother's grief has driven her to an uncharacteristic somnolence. She sleeps all day, and I can sense her dreams on my skin. She dreams of warm blood, soft feathers, strands coming loose from a long braid that tapers down to a fine point like a tail. She wakes at night to hunt in the valley, while I stay home and watch the moon rise. Its yellow grin reminds me of how Mija would smile whenever she was the first to draw blood during one of our hunts.

"Why do you let Mother scare you?" Mija used to ask me when we were children.

"I'm not like you, Mija," I would say. "It's not just Mother I'm afraid of."

I was afraid of everything in those days—the gnarled claws of old tree roots, the harsh cawing of crows, the glowing eyes of the forest creatures that watched us at night. Most of all, I was afraid of being left alone, of one day waking up to find that Mother and Mija had abandoned me and left me to fend for myself in the forest.

The world of the humans who lived in the valley below was an even more frightening prospect. Mother told us stories of greedy hunters who would skin us and wear our pelts around their necks; of bent-backed old women who would scald us in cauldrons of boiling water; of vicious young boys who would impale us with sharp sticks, tie rocks to our tails, or, even worse, cut them off completely.

But Mija was never frightened by these stories, or even by Mother herself, with all her moods and furies. "You don't have to be afraid of anything as long as I'm around, Okja," she would say, baring her teeth at me affectionately. "I'll protect you."

The first time Mija and I came across a tiger, we were just cubs. Mother had gone out to hunt, after telling us to stay close to the den. But Mija had wanted to play, to venture near the top of the mountain. We were crossing a stream, splashing each other and yelping at the coldness of the water, when we heard it—a low, rumbling growl that sounded like thunder. We looked up to see the tiger, a bright blaze of death, on the bank ahead of us. He lunged, and he would have had me in his iron jaws in a second had Mija not thrown herself between us, snarling back even though she was not a tenth of his size. The tiger sniffed, confused by the nine tails bristling behind her, and after a moment, backed away. Animals always know that we are not one of them, even if they do not spot what we are at first.

It is autumn now, and still warm. Soon it will be time for the farmers of the village to harvest their crops of buckwheat and rice. I wonder what they must make of the fact that, night after night, Mother is killing their livestock. She tears the throats out of the villagers' chickens and spills their gizzards on the ground, and she disembowels the pigs and horses, to bring home their glistening, iron-rich livers. We eat them together silently before she goes back to sleep.

I paint the outside of our den with the blood of these animals

as a warning to the villagers to stay away, but it is mostly a pre-
caution. Not even the burliest of the village farmers and hunters would dare lay a hand on my mother in her fox form, with
her gleaming teeth and claws and nine pointed tails. Mother has
killed countless men in her time, and she would not hesitate to
do so again. The only man she has ever encountered that she did
not kill was our father. She doesn't talk about him very much,
but I have decided, based on details she has let slip about him
over the years, that he must have been a wandering poet-scholar,
as gentle and wise as she is clever and ferocious. Sometimes, in
my more foolish moments, I wonder if she fell in love with him
during their time together.

"I've seen the men in the village," Mija used to scoff whenever our mother told us about the humans who lived at the foot
of our mountain. "They don't even have claws to defend themselves. What are they to us?"

"Men are weak, and slow," Mother had agreed. "But they have
weapons, and they are cunning. If a man sees you in your fox
form, he will try to kill you, thinking only of his livestock or his
family. But if you appear to him as a lovely woman, he will forget
all about his livestock, his wife, and even his children, and offer
you your heart's desire. And that," she had said, "is when you
must strike."

Kumiho are opportunistic. We can eat almost anything—
rabbits, deer, vermin—to survive, for a time. But without human
flesh, we grow weak. Our blood is fed best by the blood of men.
Mother taught us that a man's heart and his groin are his most
vulnerable parts, and that sometimes, to get to the one, we must
go through the other.

On the ninth day after Mija's death, Mother takes me to the top
of our mountain, where there is a still, small pool, fed by the

fresh mountain streams. It is, she says, where the sky-maidens who live in the clouds come to bathe at night. The waters are deeper than they seem, and she tells me that they hold traces of magic. "Is it a lot of magic?" I ask her.

"It is enough," she says. She has me wash myself in the cold, clear water, until my matted fur is soft and clean. She licks the spots behind my ears that I cannot reach, and the unexpected tenderness of this gesture makes me feel as though I am a cub again.

She studies me, her amber eyes narrowing with a hint of her old, wicked glee. "You're ready," she says. I blink, and Mother has become a woman, standing tall and straight in a worn hanbok. It is white, the color of mourning.

I realize that I have transformed as well. Kumiho can transform at will, but I do not like to see myself in human form—I know, from what Mother has told me, that I do not make a beautiful woman—and transformation is usually uncomfortable. It feels like all the bones in my body are bending and aligning themselves into the shape of a girl. These waters must be steeped in a powerful magic, to make the transformation feel as simple and natural as the changing of the leaves.

Mother rakes my hair with a wooden comb that has sharp, wide-set teeth, and I wince, both at the pain when the comb tugs through the tangles in my hair, and at the sight of my reflection in the water. My breasts are small, and my legs are like those of chickens. Mother says I have a face like a swollen moon—wide and pale and wondering—and my eyes are mismatched and unevenly spaced. Mija, as a girl, had an angular, clever face, with high cheekbones and eyes like stars, and she had a graceful figure that Mother praised for being like her own.

A water bug glides across the pool, disturbing my reflection, and when the surface stills again, I gasp. For an instant, I think that I see Mija in the water, but it is me. There are new hollows in my face, and my lips are full. My breasts are rounded and shapely, as are my arms and legs. As Mother glides the comb through my hair, I become more and more beautiful. She smooths back the loose strands with yellow oil from a glass bottle that I have never seen before and braids it into one long, polished rope down my back. When she is done, she dresses me in a hanbok the color of pale-blue dawn and tells me that I am to go down to the village tonight.

"Alone?" I ask. I am not accustomed to wearing human clothing, and the hanbok itches my underarms. I feel so much heavier, walking around on two legs. It feels ridiculous, indecent.

"The shaman whose trap killed our Mija has a son," she tells me. Her words are cold, measured. "You will meet him tonight on his way home from gathering firewood, and you will tell him that you are lost and that you need a place to stay."

I think of Mother's stories from our childhood, about the wicked hunters and village boys who will surely kill and eat me, and the blood thumps in my ears. *Afraid, afraid, afraid,* it sings to me, even though kumiho are not supposed to feel fear. Sometimes I think that Mother is right, that I took all of our father's human parts and none of her kumiho traits.

"I knew I should have killed you when you were born," Mother spits, seeing me stiffen at the mention of a man. "When you and your sister were cubs, you would never latch on to me properly when I nursed you. I thought you were sickly, did everything I could to make you drink from me. I neglected your sister because I was worried that you would not grow."

I think that she will strike me or push me into the water, and I tense and bare my teeth, surprising us both. Then Mother laughs.

"I am not the one you should be directing your rage at, Okja," she says. She continues, as though this momentary rupture has not occurred. "He will take you to his home, where you will tell the shaman and his wife that you are grateful for their hospitality. When night falls, you will kill the boy and bring me back his heart. You must do this to avenge your sister, or her restless spirit will wander this land forever."

"I've never killed a man before," I say. I see my mouth tremble in the surface of the water, and I am filled with disgust for myself. *What would Mija say?*

I raise my chin. "What must I do?"

"You may need to make him believe that you are in love with him," she says, as if it is as easy as that. "Men will believe anything when a pretty girl is saying it. But the magic of these waters will wear off in a few hours' time, and you will become a fox again by sunrise. The shaman will kill you if you are not back by then."

She sends me down the mountain with a rusty dagger tied to my underskirts and a jade pendant on a red string around my neck, to protect me against goblins and other spirits, many of whom do not love kumiho. I remember the tiger that attacked Mija and me many years ago and steel myself, but the creatures of the forest, mortal and immortal alike, keep away from me. Before I can stop myself, I think that I must tell Mija about these developments and how much she'd laugh at the idea that I am to seduce and kill a man, all on my own.

I think about what Mother said, about Mija's spirit wandering the earth. "Mija, are you there?" I whisper. "I miss you." I would give anything to hear her laugh, to feel the warmth of her breath across my face.

But I hear nothing except the sighing of the trees.

By the time I reach the outskirts of the village, the sun is low in the sky, and the air is thick with the smell of humans. It is a greasy, yet metallic smell that lingers in my nostrils, like a curse. It makes me gag, and I long for the cold winds of our mountain air. My voluminous skirt catches on a branch. I fall face first in front of a figure that I realize, much too late, is the shaman's son.

"Are you all right?" The figure shifts the bundle of firewood it is carrying and helps me to my feet.

"I'm so sorry," I murmur, remembering that I am supposed to be a lady.

He is younger than I thought he would be, and he stands as tall and straight as a young pine. His eyes are nothing like mine or Mother's—they are dark and shining and remind me of a deer's, just before it bounds away. There is a quickness in them. Perhaps it is the shaman's blood in him.

"A young lady shouldn't be wandering these woods alone after sundown," he says, in what I think is meant to be a stern manner.

"I was with my sister, gathering mushrooms, but it seems we've gotten separated," I tell him, lowering my head. "I would be so grateful if you could point me to a place in your village where I might be able to stay the night. I'm sure my sister has just gone home without me, but our village is all the way on the other side of the mountain." The lie unspools out of me smoothly. I realize how easy it is to lie when you want what you are saying to be true.

I feel his eyes search me for a stray tail or a set of claws that might give me away before they traverse the contours of my new face. I would not be the first creature of the mountain to disguise herself among humans, as my mother did once, long ago, to couple with my father. But the magic of the sky-maidens' pool is strong, and it conceals anything about me that would normally give a kumiho away, including my nine tails and yellow eyes.

"What is your name?" he asks me, and I cannot think of what to say.

"Mija," I say finally.

"Mija," he says. "I'm Yeongchul. It's dangerous in these woods after dark. My father's house does not have much room, but you are welcome to spend the night with us."

"Thank you, sir," I say, bowing once again. It is tiresome, all this bowing and standing on ceremony, I think.

"My father is a cautious man," Yeongchul says, frowning. He is clearly still trying to figure me out. "He can see things that most people cannot. But my younger sister would be your age now had she lived, and I would hate to think of her wandering on her own in the forest after nightfall."

"What happened to your sister?" I ask.

"Fever," he says shortly. He reshoulders his bundle of firewood, and we resume walking. The hem of my hanbok drags behind me in the dirt. The fox part of me wants to get down on all fours and run instead, which would certainly be much faster than bothering with these clumsy two legs.

I walk behind Yeongchul, studying the back of his dirt-streaked neck. If I were stronger, I think, like Mija, I could simply pounce on him and tear his throat out and be done with it. But the longer I stare at his neck, the more I long to reach out and touch it. The sadness in his voice when he mentioned his sister makes me want to tell him about Mija and how without her it feels like the sun is no longer as bright as it used to be. But I remember Mother's words, the reason I am here in the first place, and I harden myself.

At last, we reach the shaman's home. Bundles of herbs and

oddly shaped wood carvings hang from the eaves of the thatched roof. Yeongchul sets down his bundle of wood.

"Mother, this is Mija. She needs a place to stay for the night," he says to the kind-faced old woman standing in the doorway. The whole place is redolent of hexes. It makes my skin crawl to venture so close to them, but I grit my teeth and step inside.

The shaman is sitting cross-legged on a woven cushion and smoking a pipe. Puffs of smoke wreathe his face and beard, as though he were a dragon. I was expecting him to look fearsome, or at least dignified, but he is just an old man with thinning hair and a gray beard. His eyes widen at the sight of me.

"Who are you?" the shaman asks. I feel a stab of fear. Surely, he can see, with his second sight, what I really am.

"Father, this is Mija, from the village on the other side of the mountain. She was lost in the woods," Yeongchul says. The shaman sucks smoke from his pipe and grunts in response.

"I suppose she'll need a bowl of rice, too, then," he says. "Sit down, girl."

I realize that Mother was right, and that men, when given the choice of seeing a kumiho or a pretty girl, will always choose to see a pretty girl. I feel a strange mix of relief and disappointment.

During the evening meal, the shaman and his wife bicker pleasantly with each other, arguing over how much he eats. "You have grown fat," she tells him. "A fat shaman is no good at his trade. The ghosts and spirits will be jealous of your prosperity and refuse to listen to your prayers and commands."

"It is your fault that I have grown so fat," he scolds her, while she rolls her eyes and scoops more rice into his bowl. There is an easy warmth to their exchange, a rhythm to their loving barbs that fills me with envy and longing.

Yeongchul eats silently, only looking up occasionally to compliment his mother on the freshness of the vegetables or the plumpness of the rice cakes. Our eyes meet, and he smiles at me. I smile back, before remembering that he does not know what I am and that I have no business losing myself in his eyes, no matter how kind or steady their gaze.

The shaman's voice interrupts my thoughts. "The woods aren't what they used to be, eh, Mija?" He sits back in his seat, patting his belly with satisfaction after the meal. I am unsure of how to respond, but he continues, packing his pipe.

"When I was a boy, the woods were safe, plentiful. The waters sparkled, the air was clear, and the animals practically gave themselves over to be hunted. Now it's crawling with restless spirits, demons. No surprise, given all the strife in the land nowadays. Bound to rustle up some lower entities." A ring of smoke hangs in the air.

"Father, don't frighten Mija. She's just a girl," Yeongchul says gently.

"Don't tell me what to do, boy. Your sister was a girl, too, wasn't she?" the shaman snaps. "Don't forget, we have a duty as men to warn our women and keep them safe."

His wife's face dims noticeably at the mention of their daughter. She begins to clear the dishes. I move to help her, but she urges me to sit.

"If only your sister had been born a boy. She took more of an interest in the rituals and instruments and prayers than you ever did," the shaman continues, taking little notice of the shame on Yeongchul's face, the beginnings of a blush darkening his forehead. "Only a girl, and she could have taught you a thing or two! She had the knack."

Yeongchul looks down into his bowl of rice. "Forgive me, Father."

The shaman waves his apology away moodily. There is a heaviness in the air. "See any kumiho up there today?" he asks me, changing the subject.

"Aren't kumiho just an old wives' tale?" I say, forcing myself to laugh.

"Far from it. They're extremely dangerous," the shaman says. "There's a bad one up in the mountains, not far from here. She kills our livestock, murders the odd peddler or child who wanders too far from home. I've seen her. And there are others. Multiple fox tracks around that area."

He has been tracking us. My skin pricks all over. "I'm sure even a pack of them would be no match for you, with all your spells and protections," I say, remembering to flatter him.

"Well, Yeongchul came up with a clever plan," the shaman said, clapping his son on the back. "A poisoned snare, set with hexes. As soon as one gets infected, it gets to them all. Wipes out the whole bunch."

Yeongchul is pleased again, happy to have his achievements recognized by his father. I feel a flash of revulsion and recognition when I see the look of relief on his face at his father's praise.

"It was nothing much," Yeongchul says. "All I had to do was set the snare in the path of the kumiho we saw."

"And what did she look like?" I ask.

"Hardly the stuff of legends," the shaman says, laughing uproariously. "This one had seen better days. Mangy brown coat, fur falling out in patches. But had I come any closer, she would have torn my throat out as soon as she laid eyes on me."

The snare was for me. I was the one who was supposed to die. I nearly upset my cup of tea. "That is very clever," I say, my voice even. "Did you catch her?"

The shaman scowls. "By the time we got back up there, she

was gone. Some half-wit hunter or hermit made off with her, I suspect. No idea what they've gotten their hands on. The pelt alone, no matter how shabby, could fetch a handsome price in the markets."

I watch my tea grow cold as the shaman and his son resume talking, their voices loud and full of the easy, raucous laughter of men. I wonder what it might feel like to kill them both, right here.

That night, after the shaman and his family have gone to sleep, I lie awake on the straw pallet they have given me to sleep on in the storeroom. Mother's voice rings in my head. *I knew I should have killed you when you were born.* I wonder if she would have gone to the trouble of having Mija avenge me, had I been the one who had died as a result of the shaman's snare. I wonder if she knew that the snare had been meant for me all this time.

I sit up and slide open the door. I move, as silent as a shadow, to where Yeongchul sleeps.

When I enter his room, I feel an itching along my spine, and I turn to see if someone is gazing at me through the cracks in the walls. I wonder if, somewhere, Mother is watching and listening, to see if I will once more fail to live up to her expectations.

I kneel over Yeongchul and lift the dagger high above his throat. Mija would not even have bothered with a dagger—she would have bitten through the skin, crushed his windpipe, and drunk his warm blood greedily while his shrieks filled the house, until the shaman and his wife came running, and when they did she would have killed them, too.

Outside, an owl hoots a warning, and something small— a mouse, a baby rabbit, perhaps—screams. Yeongchul's eyes flutter open, and I lower the dagger.

"Yeonghee?" he says, his voice sleep-muddled. I realize that he must think I am his sister.

"Yeongchul, I'm sorry to wake you. I—I was frightened by a noise outside," I say, my guts twisting. "I didn't know what to do."

"Don't go outside," he says, his eyes closing again. "There's a fox out there. She's been calling me all night." My heart thuds. *Mother?*

He sighs, turns his head to the side. His light snores resume.

I wait for another minute or two before I find the courage to lift my dagger again. This time, I swear to myself, I will not waver.

The moon shines through the paper covering the windows, illuminating his face. He looks like a child, I think, before remembering that, compared with me, he is a child. Humans live for such a short time.

I wonder if he misses his Yeonghee as much as I miss my Mija. If he wishes not only that Yeonghee had lived but that she had been, as his father had said at dinner, born a boy, another son to carry on the family tradition, so that he could do something else, perhaps learn a new trade instead of making poisoned snares and hexes.

I think about the way the shaman boasted about his knowledge of us when, in fact, he knows nothing of our true natures, the depth of our powers, or how fiercely we can love. How he talked about the price of our pelts. How the shaman's wife immediately fell silent at the mention of Yeonghee, and how there is no one to help her with the chores now, how utterly alone she must feel in her grief some days, with her men out in the world and no daughter to stay at home and tend the fires with her.

I tell myself to forget this family's troubles. I know that I must strike, that I owe Yeongchul and his family nothing, and that my own mother is waiting for me at home. That Mija, my sister, the only one in the world who loved and protected me, is gone, and that it is Yeongchul and his father's fault, and that all men would root us out and kill us and sell our remains for parts until nothing of us is left.

But the dagger trembles in my hand.

Killing Yeongchul will not bring Mija back, nor will it appease her spirit, which is also gone. It will not make Mother happier, and it will never make her love me.

I sink to my knees.

In just a few hours, the sun will rise, and the magic that clings to my face and body will fade, along with my beauty. I will, once more, be an ordinary kumiho, with yellow eyes and nine tails. But I do not have to go back home, I realize. I can choose another way. Not because I am afraid to kill Yeongchul, but because killing him is what my mother would do, and I am not my mother. And for the first time in my life, I feel that this is not the worst thing in the world.

I leave the dagger behind me on Yeongchul's pallet as both a warning and a message. Somewhere in the house, the shaman snores, and his wife mutters in her sleep. I slide open the door, breathing in the freshness of the air. The trees part before me as I make my way, not upward to the top of the mountain but farther down into the valley.

I begin to run, faster and faster, shedding pieces of my hanbok along the way. I crouch down to all fours until I am bounding, leaping, my long body sinuous and free. The cool of the night feels good on my skin. I growl, my teeth lengthening and my ears sharpening. My fur covers me once more, its dapples and spots allowing me to melt into the shadows.

No goblin or tiger or hunter or shaman would frighten me

now, and the night whispers to me like a friend. I am alone and unafraid. I am half kumiho and half human—born to kill and drink the blood of men, but free to choose my own fate, and to make my own way through this life.

My eyes yellow and adjust as I plunge deeper into the night.

Mantis

The praying mantis lives in a small but well-furnished and moderately priced studio apartment in an oak tree overlooking a baseball field in the park. On warm spring days, she hears the crack of a bat and the faraway roar of a crowd she doesn't pay attention to. On weekends, she likes to stay in and read, or catch up on the latest news with a friend. Her friendships don't last very long, so the news she gets from them is always fresh, and she never has to concern herself with keeping the names and situations of their lives straight in her mind.

Lately, the mantis has felt restless, the thrill of stalking and consuming her prey—whether it be a moon-addled moth, a frisky horsefly, or a crisp ladybug—no longer as exciting as it once was. The mantis is not used to this, as she has always been driven by her desires, from the moment she wakes up till the moment she folds herself up into a green pagoda to sleep at night. But tending to these wants has grown tiring. She wonders if inside her there is only a series of jaws, daisy-chained into a flat loop of unceasing hunger. She finds herself second-guessing her decisions, listlessly contemplating her desires, and finding them uncompelling. Her increasing inability to derive enjoyment from things was something she had been working on with her therapist, a millipede with a tendency to run late, until she got fed up with his tardiness and ate him. He had been juicy yet surprisingly tough, and he had tasted like dark soil, a slightly bitter flavor she dreamt about for days afterward.

Sometimes the mantis goes on dates. She's never disappointed by the males she meets, because she never expects much from them. The sex is usually fine—adequate at best and unremarkable at worst. She enjoys the click she feels when they mount and socket themselves into her, as well as the crackling sound their heads make when she pincers her mouth around them. The males seem grateful to die while inside her, their jerking bodies moving even more frantically once she's killed them. She remembers most of these assignations, if not the males themselves, fondly.

When the mantis falls in love for the first time, it is with a male almost half her size, the same subtle green as her—a shade darker than the leaves of the oak tree. He approaches her boldly, unlike the others, who all creep up to her with the same air of mingled shame and excitement, and she is surprised by how much she likes this boldness. One of his front legs is slightly shorter than the other, and he walks with a graceful, tripping gait that she admires.

He invites her to a bar in his neighborhood, and she accepts, taking care with her appearance. They discuss themselves and the things they enjoy: the sound of birds in the morning, the tremble of the leaves in a storm, the taste of dew.

"It's too bad that all of this will end with you eating me," he says at the end of their date, when he's walking her back to her place. "I've enjoyed getting to know you."

"We don't have to do that yet," she finds herself saying. "We can continue getting to know each other."

"I don't take it at all personally," he says, almost apologetically. "I know how it goes." And he closes his eyes, in case she changes her mind and decides to end things then and there.

The mantis considers her options. Her hips swivel, ready to accommodate him, while her jaws ache to snap around his neck, to crush his eyes and pick at his flesh. But she remembers something the millipede said to her, a session or two before she ate him, about how wanting did not always have to equal having. If all you ever do is go after the things you want, you'll never know what it is you need, he'd said, and she'd wondered if she should just eat him up right then and there for saying something so stupid.

But it is late and she is feeling generous, and as the rosy August moon strawberries into the sky, she kisses him good night—she notices the twang of fear in his body when he feels the whisper of her jaws along his face—and goes inside her apartment and shuts the door, leaving him outside, and alive. She sleeps easy that night for the first time in weeks, and in the morning she catches a fat mayfly, relishing the crunch of its wings, but decides to eat only half of it, saving the rest for later. Perhaps not everything has to be consumed right away in order to be enjoyed, she thinks, proud of herself.

A few days later, his body turns up below the oak tree. Someone else has made short work of his head and thorax, and she knows that it is him by the length of one of the front legs, curled underneath the limp body. She feels an alien regret pool inside her, as fresh as rainwater, watching as a group of human children gather around the body to poke at it with a stick. She will never get to ask him his thoughts on the sound of ducks in the spring now, or about the leaping of crickets in late summer. She will never see the look of fear and awe in his acid-green eyes when she twists her head to stare into them mid-coitus. And she will never know if she would have stopped herself, kept her jaws closed, after he had been inside her; if she would have known how to enjoy his company without making him forever and irrevocably hers.

The Sound of Water

Justin had just finished watering his mother's plants when Ellie Park, eighteen years older than when he'd last seen her, walked into his family's convenience store. It was a slow summer day. A fan rotated in the corner sluggishly.

"Can I get a pack of Marlboro Lights?"

He looked up from his phone and squinted at the woman who stood in front of him. She wore sunglasses and tapped her fingernails distractedly against the countertop. A cloud of rose perfume tickled his nose.

"Ellie?" he said. He felt the back of his neck tingle as he said her name, told himself it couldn't be her. He'd last heard that she was living somewhere in New York City, maybe, or Boston, and that she was married.

She lowered her sunglasses. "Holy shit. Justin? Is that you?"

He felt himself blush as he reached for the cigarettes.

"Could you get me a lighter, too?" she said, fishing around in her purse. "White," she added, before he could ask her what color.

"On me," he said. "I can't believe you're still buying white lighters."

"Old habits die hard," she said. "And you don't have to do that." But her hands were already closing around the pack of cigarettes and the lighter he had slid across the countertop. He tried to keep his hands from trembling.

He could still remember cupping his hand around the flame of her cigarette in his parents' driveway the night she and his older brother, James, broke up, right after their high school graduation. He had been walking home from a party when she called out to him from her beat-up old Camry, her voice a little husky. When he got closer, he could see she'd been crying. "Want to go for a drive?" she said. "I could use some company." She'd offered him a cigarette as well, and he'd taken it, even though Coach Jay would kill him if he knew. The smell of Ellie's rose perfume and the clean, hot flame had made him feel dizzy.

She wore her hair shorter now, and it was tinted a reddish-gold color that didn't quite suit her. Her face had narrowed with time, and there was a slight tiredness around her eyes. But she looked good. Better than good. She still had freckles, he noticed, a small scattering of them across her cheekbones. She was the only Korean girl he'd ever seen with freckles.

"What are you doing back in town?" he asked. He wondered, with sudden self-consciousness, how he must look to her, whether she could tell his swimmer's muscles had softened over the years. He wished he had showered that morning.

"Just seeing my parents," she said, after a brief pause. "How are yours? How's James?"

He told her that James was living in San Francisco now, and if her eyes betrayed a hint of interest or regret when he mentioned that James's wife was pregnant, he couldn't tell.

"I should get going," she said. "Tell your parents I say hi."

He watched as she got into a shiny black Corolla parked outside. He could make out a small form sitting in the front seat, a boy of about eight or nine years old, and as they peeled out of the parking lot, he felt an old, familiar ache behind his ribs. A kid, he thought. It wasn't a surprise, exactly. They weren't in high school anymore. Of course Ellie had grown up, gotten married, had a kid of her own. But it felt like a reminder of something he'd been feeling increasingly lately—that everyone he'd known had grown up without him and left him behind.

"Don't ever buy a white lighter," Ellie had said the night he found her in his parents' driveway. "It's bad luck. All the members of the 27 Club had them."

"So why do you have one?" he asked, trying to be cool. Ellie's mere physical proximity made him so nervous his palms were slick with sweat.

"Same reason my lucky number is thirteen," she said. "I like to get ahead of things. If bad stuff's going to happen, I want to see it coming."

He didn't understand that at all. Wasn't the whole point of superstitions and the notion of luck in general meant to help you avoid the bad stuff, not invite it in?

There was a lot about Ellie that Justin didn't understand, including why she'd dated James in the first place. James was the golden boy, who got perfect grades without trying, and who everyone liked because he had an easy, arrogant warmth about him. And Ellie was, well, Ellie. She wasn't unpopular or disliked, exactly, but she was divisive. She worked at the bookstore in the mall, got in trouble for things like refusing to say the Pledge of Allegiance, and usually sat alone at lunch, writing poetry or reading thick books by dead philosophers. At a school Valentine's Day concert once, instead of doing a choreographed dance routine to a Top 40 hit like everyone else, she brought out her guitar and intoned into the microphone, "This is a love song about knowing when to leave," before launching into an impassioned rendition of "Fast Car." Afterward, Justin found the song on YouTube and listened to it over and over again.

As she drove along the highway, the nicotine flooding his veins made him feel the way he did during the first lap of the day. When he cut through the pool like a knife and his arms and legs churned—first slowly, as his body got used to the temperature, and then faster and faster—until the only thing he could hear was the beating of his own heart and the sound of splashing all around him.

When he got home that evening, his mother already knew all about Ellie Park being back in town. "She's getting a divorce," his mother said as she heated up kimchi jjigae for dinner. "That American husband of hers kicked her out. Imagine, at her age, and with a child, too."

Justin thought sometimes that his mother lived for only three things: Jesus, news about James, and gossip. He eyed the large acrylic painting of Christ that hung on the wall opposite the kitchen table as he ate. Jesus's gentle brown eyes, as large and liquid as a deer's, probed his. "She came by the store today," he said.

"Is that so?" his mother replied, sniffing. "That girl is trouble," she'd said when Ellie and James began dating. This was not long after Ellie was nearly suspended for turning in an art project at school that involved a 3D model of a vagina composed entirely of tampons.

"She said to tell you she says hi."

His mother softened, momentarily. "How did she seem?"

"Fine, I guess," Justin said, heaping more rice onto his plate in order to avoid meeting his mother's eyes. The last thing he needed was her ferreting out that he had a nearly two-decades-long crush on Ellie Park. "How's Appa?" he said, lowering his voice.

His father's back pain had grown worse over the last few months. The doctor, a few weeks ago, had said that it was time to consider surgery. That they had waited too long already. He'd said it disdainfully, in a way that had made Justin's hands ball up into fists inside his pockets. "How much will it cost?" Justin had asked, and the doctor demurred, saying they'd have to consult with insurance first. "Useless man," his mother muttered in Korean under her breath, and for a moment, Justin had thought she was referring to him, his own uselessness as a son, unable to pay for his father's medical care and still living at home at the age of thirty-three.

"He's sleeping," his mother said.

"We should tell James about what the doctor said. About the surgery," he said.

His mother shook her head. "Don't bother him," she said. "Your brother's going to be a father soon. He's got enough to worry about. We'll manage."

Justin stared at his plate and swallowed the rage he always felt whenever his parents talked about James like he was some far-off dignitary who was too important to be bothered with the minor details of their lives. He wanted to throw his plate against the wall. They were always shielding his older brother from bad news.

After dinner, Justin went upstairs, where he could hear the TV in his parents' bedroom. He walked past the half-open door, hesitated, and turned back. "Joonsuh-yah?" his father called.

A pool of blue light illuminated the wrinkled sheets of his

parents' bed, where his father was lying down, propped up by pillows. The room smelled of Tiger Balm and sweat. "How's your back, Appa?" Justin said. His father, grimacing, tried to sit up. He waved Justin away when he reached out to help.

"Get me the remote," he said. Justin handed it to him, and he changed the channel from the news to a fuzzy soccer game. White-and-black static rained down on the players as they ran around on a yellow-green field. James had offered to buy them a flat-screen, but their father refused to switch, saying he liked his old TV just fine. Justin settled into the armchair by the bed, and they watched the game in silence for a while.

His father scratched his armpit and yawned. "Busy day today?"

"Not really," Justin said. "New shipment came in." He forgot the word for "shipment" in Korean, and instead used the English word, feeling vaguely guilty as he did so.

His father nodded. They did not discuss what the doctor had said. "We need to sell the store," Justin wanted to say. A realtor had come by a few months ago with a business card, saying they were looking to redevelop the whole block. Justin had thrown the card out, only to retrieve it from the garbage and tuck it away in the back of his wallet a few hours later. He couldn't think of any other way they would be able to pay for the surgery and the care and physical therapy his father would need afterward, even with insurance. But he remembered how much his parents had saved up to start a store of their own, all the hours his father had put into cleaning and organizing it, caring for it like it was a third child, and he didn't say anything.

"Ellie Park came by," he said.

"Who?" his father said.

"Park Ara," he said, using her Korean name. "James's ex-girlfriend."

"Oh, the chatty one," his father said. "Isn't she married now?"

"She's getting a divorce," he said.

His father snorted. "All your generation knows is divorce," he said. "You flee at the first sign of trouble or disagreement. Back in our day, a marriage was for life."

Justin felt the urge to defend his generation to his father, but he was too tired to contradict him. "I'm going to bed, Appa," he said. He shook out two pain pills for his father from the collection of bottles by his bedside table. His father grunted his thanks, his eyes already back on the TV screen.

In his bedroom, Justin shrugged off his shirt and crawled underneath the covers. He opened his phone to find a text from his best friend, Paul. "Drinks tomorrow at McNalty's. You down?"

Justin had known Paul since they were fourteen. Paul, who used to spend days indoors glued to his gaming console, had recently gone through an extreme workout regimen and, suddenly ripped, was determined to make use of his new body and the attention it got him from women. He was always asking Justin to come out with him, and though Justin was usually too tired from working to say yes, part of him was afraid that one day Paul would stop asking.

"Sounds good," he wrote back. "Who's coming?"

Paul replied instantly, rattling off a list of names that Justin was only somewhat familiar with, guys they'd known from school or who Paul knew from work. "I'm hitting the gym early tomorrow if you wanna come," Paul said.

"I'm good," Justin wrote back, tired at the thought of it. He knew he should work out, lose the extra band of fat that had collected around his middle in recent years, but the thought of lifting weights, or, worse, running like a hamster on a treadmill streaked with other people's sweat, did not appeal to him. What he really wanted to do was to start swimming again. He missed the pull of water against his body, the quiet blue calm to be found just a few feet below the surface. But memberships at gyms with pools were expensive, and he wouldn't have the time to make use of one anyway.

The next morning, he woke up at six. It was much too early, but sleep was a lost cause. He went downstairs to make coffee. His mother had already left for the early-morning service at church, where she went every day. To his surprise, his father was sitting at the kitchen table, flipping through a stack of bills.

"Are you feeling better?" Justin asked.

His father held one of the bills up. "Why were you hiding these from me?"

"I wasn't," he said, feeling like a child. It was not quite the truth, but also not quite a lie. Justin had grown used to hiding things from his father, to protect him, he told himself. Like the time he'd found GO HOME CHINKS scrawled across the store's front window and he'd had to scrub it off, or the time a red-faced man wearing a baseball cap had casually taken a piss on the doorstep. Just unbuckled his pants and did it right there, grinning, while Justin was inside at the register. He tried to shrug away these incidents as one-off, random occurrences. He didn't want his father knowing about such things, just like he didn't want his father worrying about bills they couldn't pay.

The coffee machine gurgled and spit. His father ran his hands through what was left of his hair. "I'll be in later this afternoon," he said. "You can take the rest of the day off then."

"You should be resting," Justin said.

"I feel fine," his father said.

Outside, the sun was just starting to rise, a line of pale gold on the band of blue that made up the horizon. As he drove to the store, he remembered asking his mother, when he was a kid, why his father was going bald when other dads weren't. His mother had scolded him for being disrespectful, saying, "Your father's hair falls out because he worries so much about you boys." Ever since then, he had been haunted by any signs of his father's aging, convinced that it was all his fault. James was never to blame, of course. It was Justin who was the problem, with his poor grades, his awkwardness, his inability to make friends.

Swimming had been a last resort, a suggestion from one of his mother's well-meaning friends at church, to get him to stop holing up in his room playing video games with Paul. And to everyone's surprise, including his own, Justin had taken to swimming. To Coach Jay's frustration, he almost always finished second or third in his regional meets, even though he was the fastest on the team during practices. "You're psyching yourself out," Coach always said. "You can't look over to see what the competition is doing or look too far ahead and freak yourself out. The only thing you should be thinking about is the next breath, the next length."

But he had been good enough to get a swimming scholarship to a small private college in central Jersey, not far from home. When he received his fat acceptance packet in the mail, his father's face had flushed with pride, and his mother immediately called all of their relatives in Seoul. Even James, who was rarely impressed by anything Justin did and had gotten a full ride to UPenn, was happy for him. "Way to go, little bro," he said.

That was before his father had slipped and fallen from a ladder while changing a lightbulb at the store, severely injuring his back. Before the endless procedures and doctors' visits, and interminable calls with the insurance company that he had to make because his father was incapacitated and his mother was easily overwhelmed by the phone operators' fast, clipped English.

The buoyancy he had felt at the news that he would be able to go to college after all began to fade, and he woke every morning with a heaviness inside his chest that swimming could not dissipate. He headed off to school that fall with a pit of dread in his stomach that only grew when he realized that he was no longer the fastest swimmer on the team; he would need to work twice as hard to be half as fast as most of the kids there.

In the spring of his freshman year, when his grades began to falter and it became clear that his father would not be able to go back to working at the store anytime soon, Justin sent an email to the registrar's office to let them know that he would not be returning. It was very easy, he realized as he packed his things, to let go of a dream when it had never belonged to you in the first place. Swimming had never been something he was heading toward—it was just a way out, a shortcut to being someone other than James's weird, quiet little brother.

His parents didn't say a word when he came home and told them. His mother's eyes filled with tears, and his father left the dinner table. When he finally called his brother, who was doing a consulting internship in Boston for the summer, he was surprised to find that James was angry. "You can't just give up your own life for theirs," James said.

"Someone has to stay home with them," Justin said, a snap in his voice that he had never used with his brother before. "I'm not like you."

There was an uncomfortable pause. "I'm just saying, think this through," James said finally.

"It's already done," Justin said, before hanging up.

It's temporary, he told himself. He signed up for night classes at the local community college, spent his days at the store attempting to read textbooks that he checked out from the library. But nothing interested him. Economics, which he'd vaguely considered majoring in, seemed incomprehensible, as did history, which he'd enjoyed in high school. And one year became two, became three, became five, until he stopped counting.

The next time he saw Ellie Park, it was Friday night, and she was requesting a song at McNalty's, while Paul was yelling into his ear about some Tinder girl he was seeing.

It was dark and loud in the bar. McNalty's had been an old-fashioned Irish pub that had languished for years on the corner of Broad and Myrtle, before its owner finally sold it to a Korean businessman, who had tried to turn it into some kind of night-club cum karaoke bar but had, for some reason, kept the name. The back had been converted into private karaoke rooms, from which Justin could hear the occasional rap song or ballad being shouted into feedback-prone microphones.

McNalty's was not the kind of place Justin would have picked for a night out with friends. Not that he had many friends now; he'd lost touch with most of them over the years. The guys who had joined him and Paul nodded perfunctorily at him before they began talking among themselves. Justin looked around and caught sight of Ellie. She was wearing dark lipstick and a sleeve-less black T-shirt, her phone tucked into the back of her jeans. She propped up her elbows on the bar as she gave the bartender her song request, before walking with her drink back to her table, where a pack of her girlfriends were holding court.

"Dude, you're not even listening to me," Paul said.

"Sorry," Justin said. "Long week." But Paul had caught where Justin was looking. He whistled. "Ellie looks good," he said. "Didn't know you were into older chicks."

"She's barely two years older than us," he said. But Ellie had always given off an air of being much older than everyone else, in the way she tended to look right through guys she thought weren't worth her time.

Paul gave him a sly look. "How long's it been, bro? You get any since you and what's-her-name broke up?"

The last girl Justin had seen regularly, Melody, had broken up with him via text a few months ago, after she had gotten back together with her ex. He'd felt a blip of sadness, before feeling numb and somewhat relieved. "Melody. And none of your business."

"So no, then," Paul said, sighing.

The first few bars of an eighties synth melody came on, and Ellie squealed. She ran out onto the small stage at the center of the bar, dragging a friend with her. "Her hair is Harlow gold," Ellie sang into the mic, swaying a little. A crowd began to gather around them. Justin felt slightly anxious, the way he always did when someone sang in public, but Ellie seemed at ease with the attention. An errant spotlight danced off her shoulders and collarbones as she sang.

"Didn't she use to go out with your brother?" Paul said. "Why'd they break up?"

"I don't know," Justin said, his voice testy. Ellie had told him, in the car that night, that James said it wouldn't make sense for their relationship to continue on into college. That they had diverging futures ahead of them, because he was heading to UPenn, while she was taking a year to continue working at the bookstore and figure out what she wanted to do. "I need to be with someone who has a plan for their life," he'd told her. It was just like James, Justin thought, to try to five-year-plan his way out of an actual breakup conversation.

"Go talk to her already," Paul said.

In the end, it was Ellie who approached their table. "Hey, boys," she said, dropping her phone by accident. Justin picked it up for her, catching a quick glimpse of her lockscreen. It was a photo of Ellie and her son, sitting side by side. He had light-brown hair, almost blond, and light-brown eyes, but he had her smile, and her freckles.

"You were good up there," Justin said as he handed her the phone. "Like, really good."

"Thanks," she said. "I'm going out for a smoke, if you want to come."

"Uh, sure," Justin said, then turned to Paul, who was suddenly deeply engrossed in his phone.

"You all go ahead," Paul said, not looking up from a text he was drafting. "Good seeing you, Ellie."

"What's up with him?" Ellie said to Justin once they were outside. It was still warm out, but after the cold air-conditioning inside, the balmy night air felt like a relief.

"He's got some Tinder date he's meeting up with," Justin said. Ellie lit a cigarette. "You want one?" she said.

"A Tinder date?" he asked, confused.

She laughed. "A cigarette."

"Oh, sorry. I'm good." He tried not to stare as she took a drag and closed her eyes, savoring the taste of the smoke. She opened her eyes and smiled at him, and he felt his face grow warm. "I promised my kid I'd quit," she said.

"What's his name?" Justin asked.

"Quinn," she said. Justin wasn't conscious of having made a face until she burst out laughing again. She had beautiful teeth. "I know, I know. White-ass name. I don't know what I was thinking, but his dad liked it. It's a family name, on his mom's side."

"It's a nice name, just not one I'd expect from you," he said.

"Yeah, well," she said, her smile fading, "a lot of life is doing things you never imagined you'd do, until you've done them and you're, like, 'I guess it's too late to change that now.'" The red light of the neon sign above their heads illuminated her cheekbones and made the shadows of her eyelashes even darker.

She asked him how things were going with the store, his parents. He told her a version of the truth—that his father had never fully recovered after his fall, that they had asked him to come home. It was easier to tell this version of the story, a version in which he came home because he had been needed, not because he had been too scared to try to fight to stay at school, to insist on his right to stay.

"I'm sorry," she said, sounding genuinely sad. "I was convinced you were headed for the Olympics."

"Nah," he said, "I was never that good."

"I'm probably moving back here, too," she said. "Isn't it funny? So many of us were so desperate to get out of this town, to make something of ourselves. To have better lives than our parents, because that was the point of it all, right? Of them coming here in the first place? And then we wind up back here again." She was drunker than she had seemed in the bar. She crossed her arms and squinted up at the neon sign.

"I'm sorry about the divorce."

"I guess everyone's heard by now," she said. "It's fine. People get divorced all the time."

"What happened?" he asked.

"Oh, you know. The usual. We got tired of each other, hurt each other. He found someone new. Younger, easier. Said he wanted to give us both a chance to start over, to live our own lives."

"I'm really sorry," he said.

"Oh, shut up," she said. Then her eyes widened. "Sorry. I didn't mean that. I'm drunk."

"It's okay," he said. "It was a dumb thing to say."

"No, it wasn't," she said. "You were being nice. Nice is good." She began to cry then, looking away from him, her lit cigarette in her right hand while she dabbed at her eyes with her left wrist. He wanted to reach out and touch her, comfort her somehow, but he just stood there like an idiot.

"You know, I haven't talked to any of those girls in there for two years?" she said. "They were all bridesmaids at my wedding."

"Why not?" he said.

"Too scared to tell them about how everything was going wrong in my life," she said. "I didn't even tell my parents what was happening, until it was all over. Isn't that awful?" She was standing so close to him now that he could smell her rose perfume, see the smudges of eyeliner that had collected below her eyes.

"I don't think so," he said. "There are a lot of things we don't tell other people. Maybe you didn't want to worry them." He thought of how his mother had told him not to tell his father the worst of what the doctor had said—that, although it was the best course of action for addressing the chronic pain, there was a small chance that the surgery could impair his ability to walk, forever. That there was also a chance the procedure wouldn't do much for his back anyway. He considered all the times he had chosen silence, everything that he had never said or that had never even occurred to him to say—to his parents, to James, to himself.

She looked at him, taking in what he had said. Her eyes looked wet, bruised. "I think that was part of it," she said.

"Sometimes not telling people things can be a way of trying to protect them," he said, thinking of his mother and her reluctance to tell James about his father.

"Will you take me home?" she said, after a moment. "I probably shouldn't be driving."

The drive to her parents' house didn't take very long, but Justin was hyperconscious of every bend and turn in the road. Ellie rolled down the window, and they listened to the chirp of night insects, the rush of other cars. A passing moth tried to come inside, and Ellie caught it in her hands and pushed it gently out the window.

"My mom used to tell me that moths were the ghosts of little kids," she said. "I believed her too, for the longest time. I tried to save them all. Cried when they flew into lamps or candles."

"My mom told me that the tooth fairy wouldn't give me money for my teeth, because she didn't come to Korean kids."

"My sister told me that if you stand in the middle of a dark room at three a.m. and throw a pencil over your shoulder, you won't hear it land, because the ghost behind you catches it."

"James used to tell me that they found me under a bridge when I was a baby. Said if I was bad they'd send me back there."

"James said that? What a jerk," she said, laughing.

They slowed to a crawl in front of her parents' house. He wondered how many times James must have dropped her off after dates. If they'd had to park farther away first, before she had to sneak in.

"Thanks," she said. "Sorry I'm a bit of a mess tonight." She gave him a half-smile, like she wasn't sure whether to be embarrassed or not.

He cleared his throat and looked away. "It's okay." She was so close he could hear the quiet rhythm of her breath. He wished, not for the first time in his life, that he was someone different, someone like Paul or James, who would know exactly what to say next.

He felt her hand against his face. Her fingers were cold. Her thumb traced the edge of his cheekbone as she moved his hair away from his face tenderly, as he imagined she might do to her son. "Take care of yourself, Justin," she said.

She climbed out of the car. Just before she shut the door, she turned around and peered in at him. "It's your life, you know," she said. "Even if it doesn't feel like it is. Even if it feels like you owe your family everything. You're the one who's living it." She said it sternly, almost angrily.

"I know," he said.

He watched her walk inside. A curtain moved in the front window, and he saw two small eyes peek out to stare at him—the kid, waiting up for her. They regarded each other solemnly, until the boy closed the curtains.

The forecast on the radio threatened rain, but the skies stayed clear. He took the highway home, passing shuttered businesses, empty mall parking lots. He passed a church with a sign that read, COME AS YOU ARE. YOU CAN CHANGE INSIDE. He passed an antiabortion billboard that read, CHOOSE LIFE. PRAY PRAY PRAY. He passed a McDonald's with a sign that read, MCRIB LEAVING US SOON. ACT NOW.

The next day, he woke up early again. He stretched, felt a dry sourness in his mouth, and got up to pee and brush his teeth.

Downstairs, his father was sitting at the kitchen table. "You got in late last night," he said.

"Just met up with some friends," Justin said as he turned on the stove, then reached for a skillet and swirled oil onto its surface. He cracked two eggs into a bowl, whisked them together before pouring them into the skillet, and watched as the circle of translucent yellow coalesced into soft curds. It was James who had taught him how to make scrambled eggs, who had in fact made them for dinner often, on days when both their parents had to work late. For all his superiority, James was a patient teacher, and he had shown Justin how to crack two eggs with one hand.

"It's good to enjoy time with your friends while you're young," his father said.

Justin remembered what Ellie had told him last night. How his life was his own. But what about his father's life, or his mother's? Didn't they have lives of their own as well?

He watched as his father stood up slowly to clear the table of his own breakfast. "Appa," he said, "we need to sell the store."

"What are you talking about?" his father said.

"Your back," he said. "We can't pay for the surgery otherwise." His father didn't turn around. Outside, a cardinal landed, with a scarlet shudder, in one of the trees in their backyard, where his mother had hung a bird feeder. He couldn't remember the last time he'd seen a cardinal.

"Don't you think I know that?" his father said, his voice suddenly low and angry. He tossed the dishes into the sink and ran water over them. "You think it's so easy to give up on something. You have no idea what it's like to start from nothing, to build something solid, only to have to give it all away." A fork jangled to the ground, and although Justin made a move to pick it up, his father reached for it first, then winced as he braced himself against the counter.

"Appa, the doctors said—"

"I know what the doctors said."

Justin sat there, frozen, as he realized that his father, the man he had never seen so much as shed a tear, even when his own parents had died, was trying not to cry. He stood up. He placed a hand on his father's shoulder and felt conscious of just how much taller he was now than him. He still remembered the day he first noticed that he had grown past his father's height, and how being able to look down at the top of his father's balding head had made him feel as though he were doing something wrong.

"A man should be able to provide for his family," his father said finally. They were both staring at the cardinal now, which flitted from branch to branch.

"You have," Justin said. He cleared his throat, to get the squeak out of it. "But you have to let us take care of you now."

The drive to the store usually took around ten minutes. But just before the turnoff, Justin swung his car left, flying past the Dunkin' Donuts and the auto-body shop where his father and the owner used to swap friendly jabs with each other and haggle over repair costs. Almost without realizing it, he found himself driving toward his high school.

Dew darkened the toes of his canvas sneakers as he walked through the grass to get to the side door by the gym. It was a Saturday, so he was surprised to find the door was open. A custodian, maybe, who'd forgotten to lock up.

He walked up and down the empty varnished halls, marveling at how little the school had changed since he was a student. He even caught glimpses of his own blurred face in the framed photos of sports teams that lined the main hallway. In one, he was holding a trophy that proclaimed him the first-place winner in the one-hundred-yard butterfly, the year his school had hosted the North Jersey regional meets. It was one of the few times he'd won first place in anything.

The pool, a glowing blue rectangle bisected by a streamer of yellow and black flags, was just as he had remembered it. Lines of light from the water reflected off the walls. It was odd having an entire pool to himself, without the sounds of a whistle blowing in the background or of splashing. He sat down, slipped his shoes off, and dipped his feet into the water. The cold enlivened him, the smell of the chlorine activating a part of himself he had long forgotten.

He closed his eyes and remembered how his cheeks and shoulders had stung for hours after that win, from all the smiling he'd done for photos and the congratulatory back slaps he'd gotten from his teammates and Coach Jay. How his parents had stood up in the bleachers to cheer him on, and how he could hear his father, loudest of all, shouting his name as he raced toward the end. But most of all, he remembered how his arms and legs had seemed to lengthen as he swam. How he'd felt his pulse quicken, then slow, until the only sound he could hear was his own breath as it took on the rhythm of the water, rising and falling, again and again.

He didn't know if he would ever feel that kind of exhilaration again—not just from winning, but from how purposeful he had felt, how his mind and body had been in perfect sync. He would never again be the promising young athlete who might someday swim in the Olympics. He was just himself, as he had always been—the son who had stayed, because he hadn't been smart enough or successful enough or strong enough to make it on his own.

But it didn't matter anymore. There was no point in lingering on what had or hadn't happened. There was only what lay ahead.

He swung his legs out of the pool, shook the water off as best as he could, slipped his shoes back on. He began to make a mental list of all the things he would do that day. He would sweep the store, wipe down the windows. Stock new drinks. Order more cigarettes, batteries, potato chips. Call that realtor. Call the insurance company and the doctors, not giving up until someone gave him answers.

It was not so very much to look at, this life of his, he thought as he left the school and made his way back to the car. But it was still, and always would be, his own.

Attachment Processes

Elly came back to us at five years old, exactly the way she had been before. She was asleep in the back seat of the car when they brought her to us, her hair pulled back and up into a fountain of silky strands, held together by a red elastic. How I had loved to brush and braid her hair, to watch it shine a reddish gold in the sunlight the way my own never had.

"She'll be asleep for another five hours or so. Bootups, just to make sure all the applications are finalized," the tech said, busying herself with a clipboard. I wobbled my name onto the dotted line of the release form while Dan unbuckled the carrier and brought her inside.

"You'll need to log your progress with Eleanor over the next few months, but for now, just focus on bonding with her. She'll be learning along with you," the tech said, giving us a warm, professional smile.

"Elly," I said. "Her name is Elly."

The tech consulted her clipboard. "Of course," she said. "Elly."

The warm smile came back. "Congratulations on this exciting new journey."

"We really appreciate all the work you've put into this," Dan said, shaking her hand. He always knew just what to say, even when I didn't. It was one of the reasons we were still married.

Then it was just the three of us. We studied her as she slept, holding each other in a way we hadn't in a long time. She sighed and turned her head, revealing a small crosshatch imprint on her cheek from the fabric of the carrier. It was all so real. I bit the soft part of my palm, the web of skin between my thumb and index finger, to keep from hyperventilating.

"Andy," Dan said. His hand made circles on my back in a way that was meant to be soothing. I shrugged him off, and his hurt filled the room like a smell.

"Sorry," I said, not looking at him. "I just need a second." I bent over the carrier. I didn't know if I was afraid that they had gotten a crucial detail wrong or afraid that they had gotten everything right. But it was all there. Her long, thick eyelashes (Dan's—mine slanted straight down), the wide nose (mine, unmistakably), the perfect bow of her lips (who knew where that had come from), and the small scar over her left eyebrow from the time she had walked into our coffee table at age two.

"Let's get her upstairs," Dan said. He delicately picked her up from the carrier, supporting the back of her head as carefully as he had done when she was an infant. I followed him up the stairs obediently, helpless to understand the rising tide of grief and guilt inside me. Shouldn't I have been ecstatic? Wasn't this what every parent who had ever lost a child wanted? This was our Elly, our baby, come back to us, and all I could do was stand in the darkened hallway and bite my lips to keep from crying out.

The counselor assigned to our case had warned us that the feelings we would experience upon seeing Elly again could be confusing and difficult to process. "Reengagement is not an easy step for most families," she had said during our last session with her.

The interior of her office was tasteful yet unmemorable, in a way that I both didn't trust and felt grateful for. White walls, green plants, pale-blond furniture, and a pink rug beneath our feet. We sat on a low couch and held hands, discussing options. We could have been in any therapist's office in the world.

"You will be feeling many different, seemingly contradictory feelings, and I want you to understand that it is natural to feel afraid or upset." The counselor's voice was as smooth and mellifluous as the cello music playing in the background. "Over the next few weeks, you'll be expected to note how Elly is adjusting to life in your household. If she is remembering details, names, places."

"I thought the technology would take care of all that," Dan said.

"It will, but the embedded memories may take some time to activate," the counselor said. "The archive you provided was quite extensive, so I have no doubt that she will have everything she needs to start her new life. But you will need to be patient while the two of you—and Elly—adjust and recalibrate to one another."

"But what if she doesn't?" I said.

"Andy—"

"Dan, let Andrea express herself. This is a safe environment." I wanted to roll my eyes, but I controlled myself and took a deep breath.

"You said *if* she is remembering details, names, places. So what *if* she doesn't? What then? What if things don't go according to plan? This all seems incredibly uncertain to me."

"Isn't that the question all parents face when they're about to meet their child for the first time?" the counselor said. "Parenting is one of the most uncertain games out there," she added gently, as if I didn't already know. I studied the weave of her expensive-looking olive-green sweater and didn't say anything else for the rest of the session.

On the drive home that day, I asked Dan if he was sure.

He took one hand off the steering wheel and ran it through his hair, sighing. "We've talked about this, Andy," he said. "We've weighed the pros and cons."

"What if she hates us?" I said. "What if it's not her?"

"It won't be the same," he said simply. "But we might as well try."

He reached for my hand. His felt warm and dry, not like mine, which was damp with perspiration. When we first started dating, I had been terribly self-conscious about how sweaty my hands got, often wicking them down the sides of my dress when I thought Dan wasn't looking, but he never seemed to care. It was always me who pulled away first, worried he'd be repulsed by the slickness of my palms.

The sun was low by the time we got home. Before I got out of the car, I closed my eyes, imagining what it would be like to turn around and see her again in the back seat. When Elly was an infant, we had to put her in the car to lull her to sleep, and sometimes, as soon as we had parked the car back in our driveway, she'd bolt awake, her round eyes laughing at us in the rearview mirror as if to say, "Gotcha!"

"Okay," I said to Dan.

"Okay, what?"

"Okay, let's see," I said, trying to smile.

He gave me a grateful look. Dan, a classic middle child, hated conflict and disagreement. "Lapsi is the best in the field, Andy. We're in good hands."

It was true that Lapsi was one of the biggest and best-funded companies in the burgeoning field of thanatorobotics, though it was only three years old. There had been the usual media storm when it first opened its doors, with pundits on both the right and the left denouncing its intended mission, which was to reconstruct the deceased using the most sophisticated artificial-intelligence and consciousness-upload techniques—for therapeutic purposes only, the marketing copy stressed. The CEO and founder, a young robotics genius named Irene Nakamoto, had been fired and then rehired by the Board over the furor.

I had studied Irene Nakamoto's bio and photos online, and I knew her story almost as well as I knew my own. She was only five years younger than me. As a doctoral student in the engineering program at Stanford, she had developed a prototype that featured slices of consciousness from her deceased twin brother, Terence, who had died of leukemia when they were twelve. According to the *Time* cover story, she had managed to convert old audio and video recordings, drawings, and homework assignments of her brother's into a code that she used to create a framework for an artificial brain that, she claimed, would learn and develop over time with increased interactions, eventually becoming a duplicate of the deceased person's core consciousness. However, the technology was not yet advanced enough to rebuild the memories and synaptic structures of an adult mind. Lapsi could only create models of the minds of children, up to the age of sixteen.

The original prototype for Terence Nakamoto was displayed

in a glass case in the bright white lobby of Lapsi headquarters. Even though it was unsophisticated by today's standards—the skin detailing on the prototype was patchy and uneven in pigmentation, and the voice was slightly robotic in its cadences—Terence, or Terence Two, as the media called him, was convincing enough to gain Lapsi millions of dollars in funding from private investors. Terence Two could converse about the weather, tell you about all his favorite TV shows or classes at school, and even tell jokes.

That night, after our last counseling session, a week before Elly was due to arrive, I waited till Dan had fallen asleep before I turned on my computer. I logged on to Lapsi's website, where, for what must have been the two hundredth time, I watched the company's introductory video, in which Irene Nakamoto, wearing rimless glasses and a strong-shouldered blazer that looked like a plate of armor, gave her spiel. "Lapsi is more than just another robotics company," she said while soft, upbeat music played. "Lapsi is about giving you and your family another chance, to make things right." Then the company's tagline—in round coral lettering—flashed across the screen: "Lapsi. Because life doesn't have to end at death."

"That's a terrible tagline," I remarked when Dan first showed me the ad. It was four months after the accident. "Of course life ends at death. That's why it's called death."

But I kept coming back to the ad, again and again. Perhaps it was because of the steely glint behind Irene Nakamoto's glasses, the look of a woman who, behind the publicity hoopla, actually knew what she was doing; perhaps it was the strange rush of emotions that I felt at seeing another Asian woman, similar in age to me, doing something almost unimaginable; perhaps it was the crushing sadness that woke me every morning with its weight. But it was probably the fact that, earlier that day, on a jog, I had seen a mother and her teen daughter walking side by side and arguing, before one of them made a joke and they dissolved into twin peals of laughter, suddenly looking like sisters. The twist of pain I felt almost brought me to my knees, as the knowledge that I would never see Elly again radiated through my skull like heat.

So in the end I was the one who called the number. I did the research on Irene Nakamoto and stared at countless publicity photos of her and her parents with Terence Two, their arms around one another, grinning like a real family. I scheduled the initial consultation session, and I sketched out the hefty payment plan and managed, over months of careful campaigning, to convince Dan we should go for it.

So why did I feel, suddenly, so scared?

I had not wanted to be a mother.

Years ago, we had moved from New York City to San Francisco because Dan had snagged a UX researcher role at an up-and-coming tech company. The salary, even after accounting for the higher cost of living in San Francisco, made us both laugh with disbelief. We became obsessed with Zillow listings, the idea of living in a house with a backyard suddenly irresistible after years of being crammed into a creaky one-bedroom in Brooklyn. And along with these fantasies came another one.

About a week before we were to move to San Francisco, I woke one morning, wet-eyed, from a dream about a little girl. I had been holding her in my arms and walking, block after block, in a deserted version of our neighborhood. She had grown heavier and heavier with every step, but I knew that she was my responsibility, and that to let go of her would mean the end of both of us.

"What do you think it means?" I asked Sarah, my oldest New

.York friend. She lived in an inherited apartment in the East Village that was filled with crystals and taxidermied animals.

"That's a pregnancy dream if I've ever heard one," Sarah said. "Have you taken a test?" I scoffed at this, until I realized that my period was late.

When the two pink lines on the test confirmed that I was indeed pregnant, Dan was ecstatic. I was less so. He had always wanted kids. I had not planned on a baby. I was going to work on my book in San Francisco, finally giving up my freelance writing gigs, because Dan and I had decided that his new salary would be enough to cover us for a year or so without my working. But as time went by, it became easier to imagine a child, a small human that would look like us and eventually, we hoped, become something better than the two of us combined.

Eight months later, on a cold, foggy August day, Elly was born, and I fell in love.

Dan, of course, loved Elly as well, and, as I had always known he would be, he was a good, attentive father. But my reaction took us both by surprise. Sarah called me often in the months after Elly was born, concerned that I would be going stir-crazy with nothing but the book and the baby to keep me occupied, but I could have stared at her seashell ears, the delicate whorl of hair at the top of her tiny baby skull, and her pearlescent, rounded cheeks for hours. I told Sarah this, and she was both alarmed and amused. "Never thought you'd be *that* type of mom," she said.

We named her Eleanor, after a dead grandmother on Dan's side of the family, but it wasn't long before she became Elly, which, conveniently, could be used as a Korean name as well—Aeri. No matter how many times I taught Dan how to say it properly, with just the slightest trill over the "r," he was unable to master the pronunciation. Normally, this would have irritated me, but my happiness made me selfish, and I was secretly glad that being able to correctly say Elly's name in Korean was something he would not be able to share with me. The joy I felt when I held her or watched her observe the world felt like an iridescent, fleet-footed thing. I knew that I had done nothing to deserve its presence in my life, but I was content to let it wander through the fields and valleys of my heart. I kept waiting for this happiness to leave me, to be replaced by the inevitable postpartum depression. But, to my surprise, it lingered, took root, and grew.

As the months went by, my calls with Sarah got shorter, and gradually I stopped responding to her texts, which seemed less interesting to me as Elly began achieving milestones like sitting up, rolling over, smiling, and calling out to us, even when we were in the same room with her, just to hear the sound of her own voice.

"Have you heard from Sarah lately?" Dan asked me sometimes. Or, "I can watch Elly if you want to get out of the house for a bit." But life outside of our daughter had ceased to appeal to me. Elly was growing up so quickly, despite my best efforts to pause time, to will the days and hours and minutes to slow down.

My agent called to check in about the book. "If you need more time, just let me know," she said carefully. I was writing a narrative history about the haenyo—female sea divers—of Chejudo, but the writing was not going well. I told her I needed more time.

Instead, I turned my energies toward teaching Elly Korean, pointing to household objects and repeating their names. I pointed to myself—"Umma"—and to Dan—"Appa." She giggled and mimicked me, thinking it was a game. Although I never succeeded in getting her to call me "Umma," Elly did learn the Korean phrase for "I love you," and for some reason, she used it exclusively for attempting to get out of trouble. "Mommy, saranghae," she said when she was caught drawing on our white walls with crayon or unspooling all the toilet paper off the roll.

When she got older, I told her about the haenyo. My grandmother had been the last haenyo of our family, a spry, tan woman who, according to my mother, could plunge up to thirty meters deep, holding her breath for minutes at a time, to emerge with bounties of abalone, sea urchins, oysters, and conch. "Like a mermaid," Elly said. She pretended to be a haenyo in the tub, often asking me to time her while she held her breath.

When she started school, it became too difficult to counteract all the new English words she was learning every day. I thought guiltily of what my parents would have said, had they known that their only grandchild knew so little Korean. But they had died in a car accident years ago, when I was in my senior year of college.

The darkness I felt during the years following their deaths felt apocalyptic. When I met Dan, I had already tried to kill myself twice. The first time with pills, but then I called a roommate. The second time, a kind stranger called a hotline for me while I was pacing on the George Washington Bridge and trying to make up my mind.

Once Elly started elementary school, I went back to the book, which took three years to finish, and another year to sell. We celebrated at our favorite restaurant, a Mexican place, where I drank my first margarita in years; the salt and tequila coursed through my bloodstream so rapidly that I almost burst into tears at the sight of Dan and Elly, the family I had managed to build for myself after so many years of being alone.

Things weren't always easy. Elly could be frustrating. She threw magnificent tantrums, with wails as loud as sirens.

But she was also strange, and smart, and funny. Before bed-time, she had conversations with beings I could not see, which she called "the angels." She related their stories and adventures to me in a low voice, warning me that I couldn't tell anyone else, but that the angels had told her it was okay to tell Mommy. Some-times she put on all the dresses she owned to play a mysteri-ous game called "opera" that mostly involved her standing at the top of the stairs and belting Celine Dion. She collected rocks and acorns and left them around the house in careful, deliberate arrangements that she called "museums."

As the days went by, my happiness gradually became a steady, dependable thing, a presence with heft and volume, and I no longer woke up anticipating its leaving me in the night, like a faithless lover. Now that I had Elly, I knew that my days of lone-liness and my endless seeking for something to fill the gnawing spaces inside me were over.

The night Elly came back to us, I studied the materials the tech had provided. The glossy brochure, the testimonials, the instruc-tional booklet. I knew them all by heart.

Grief is a lifelong process, and Lapsi is meant only to be a stop-gap for processing that grief, said the first page. In one of the many interviews I read featuring Irene Nakamoto, she said that she missed her brother so much that she used to spread his clothes out on his bed and pretend he was lying there while she told him about her day, and it had brought her a kind of comfort that no amount of grief counseling or therapy could.

Remember that your Lapsi will require time and sustained interaction in order to be fully integrated into your day-to-day life. Your Lapsi is learning along with you. This was a strange, sad echo of something that our midwife had told us, in the months before Elly came. "It's amazing how much babies know already when they come out," she said. "But it's up to you to interact and learn along with your baby, too."

It is not recommended that you explain to your Lapsi the circumstances of their background, as it could inhibit the attachment processes essential to kickstarting your Lapsi's behavioral learning. "When I first developed Terence Two," Irene Nakamoto said during an interview on *60 Minutes,* "I tried to tell him what had happened to him, but he couldn't understand, and while the scientist in me balks, of course, at saying this, or of ascribing emotionality to tech generally, I felt that he was sad. It inhibited how quickly he was able to understand basic conversation structures or mimic Terence's thought patterns."

Lapsi is committed to providing you with the highest quality of care and service. Thank you for being part of our community.

"Mommy?"

People use the expression "My heart skipped a beat," often without thinking too much about what that could mean. It felt, in that moment, as though my heart had simply stopped working. But my body remembered what to do, and it propelled me out of bed and down the hallway to Elly's room.

"I had a bad dream." She was sitting up, her hair mussed in its fountain. Her cheeks were as red as they always used to get after a long nap. Had she always had that tendency to rub first one eye, then the other? Or was this a variation that Lapsi had introduced to her code?

"I'm here," I said, as stiff as an actor who has forgotten her lines. I gathered her into my arms. "What was your dream about?" I said.

"I dreamt that I was underwater." She looked up at me and frowned. "Why are you crying, Mommy?"

"It's nothing. Tell me about your dream, baby."

She smiled at me, and it was a wonder. They had gotten her smile exactly right, down to the dimple that appeared in her right cheek and the way her eyes narrowed and her nose flared slightly, just like mine.

"I dreamt that I was lost, and it was so cold. But then the angels came and told me to swim up, and I did, and you were there."

I held her tighter. The angels in Elly's dreams had never unsettled me before, but now they seemed sinister. I did not like to think about what combination of genetic mapping and image sequencing Lapsi must have engineered to ensure that this Elly would have the same recurring dreams.

"Umma," she said, and I almost recoiled. She had never called me "Umma" before.

The next day was Saturday. We took Elly to a park a few towns away, where we were unlikely to run into anyone we might know. It felt odd to strap her into her car seat once again, to wrap the seatbelt around its base and buckle it into place, a task that had seemed maddeningly complex when she was a baby.

We watched her climb up and down the jungle gym and slide down every slide. I watched her for more signs of slippage, looking for holes in Irene Nakamoto's code. I had barely slept the night before, and I felt feral with renewed grief.

"It's not her," I said.

"We knew that going into this," Dan said. "That isn't the point."

"I don't even remember why we did this. It just feels wrong. She's not even a child."

"She can feel things, right? She can respond to stimuli, to questions. And we are still responsible for her. We helped create her and bring her into the world," Dan said. He looked tired, older.

Not for the first time, I wondered why on earth he had married me. He deserved to be with someone uncomplicated and beautiful, someone with a name like Bethany or Kaitlin. A nice, smooth-haired girl who would never have let what had happened to Elly happen.

"It's going to be okay," he said. "We'll just have to wait and see how things go."

"Umma, Daddy! Watch me!" Elly shrieked as she waved, one-handed, from the monkey bars. No one could have known, from watching us, what she really was.

"What are we going to tell our friends?" I asked. "We'll have to tell them soon. They'll think we're monsters. They'll want to know why."

"We'll tell them that we're just trying this out, that it's been proven to be very effective as grief therapy. Everything we're doing is perfectly understandable."

"What if I can't get this right? What if I screw up a perfectly functional child robot, too?"

"Don't think like that," Dan said. "What happened wasn't your fault."

Elly was sixteen when she died. There is not much I can say about this other than that, when they told me the news, I thought I would die, too. I had been working on my second book then, and afterward I was completely unable to write.

I could count the number of times my parents told me they loved me on one hand, so I told Elly how much I loved her all the time. Parenting is a kind of revision, I suppose. A reworking of what you have been taught to think and believe, calibrated for an entirely new person that never asked to be part of your psychodrama. And what is a family but a group of people who agree to believe in these revisions together, to pretend that they do not see the small cracks and fissures where the stories do not quite align?

In middle school, Elly began cheating on her tests and homework. Her teacher required all tests to be signed, and she came home with a 65 on a math test, which she had disguised as an 85 with the curve of a pen. I asked her how it was possible that she had received an 85 when she had gotten so many of the answers incorrect, and she burst into tears and refused to answer me when I demanded to know why she had lied.

"You're smarter than this," I told her, thinking I was being encouraging.

She began bringing home new pens, erasers, even a red pencil-case in the shape of a cat. "Where did you get these things?" I asked, and she told me that they were presents from her friends. It wasn't until I got a call from her teacher saying that Elly had been stealing things from her classmates' desks that it occurred to me to wonder what else Elly had been lying to me about.

It got worse as Elly grew older. She developed unsavory friends, including a pale-eyed girl named Marina whom I detested, who reeked of cigarettes and never said hello. Elly skipped classes, stopped handing in her homework, started talking back to us during arguments. I tried coaxing, discipline, heart-to-hearts about what was going on, but none of it worked. The little girl who had insisted on being the one to tell me bedtime stories at night was gone, leaving a sullen, withdrawn, and lank-haired teenager in her wake.

Dan tried to intervene, to play good cop to my bad cop. She yielded sometimes to his overtures, agreeing to be taken out for ice cream and given gentle lectures on her behavior. But with me, she was closed off, silent. "I don't know why she can't just leave me alone," I overheard her say to Marina once on the phone. "She wants me to be exactly like her. It's exhausting."

She came home late one night from an alleged study session smelling like smoke and beer. "Where have you been?" I said when she walked in the door. She froze, before relaxing her face into the contemptuous composure she had learned over the last few years.

"At Marina's. I'm tired, Mom—"

"Try again. Where have you been? You were supposed to be home two hours ago, at ten. It's midnight."

"I told you—"

"If you wanted to go to a party, why wouldn't you just tell me you wanted to go to a party? Why would you lie to me?"

"Because I knew you wouldn't let me go! Because you never like me to go out and have fun with my friends! You want me to stay at home all the time, just like you."

"What is wrong with you?" I found myself screaming at her. "Do you think I'm stupid?"

She gave me a look full of venom. "I hate you," she said, and my heart closed like a door. I reeled with the pain of seeing my daughter want to hurt me.

Later that week, Elly called home at around 5:00 p.m. She had told us that morning that she would be staying after school to work on a group project, and that she would get a ride back home with one of her project partners. So I ignored the call, letting it go to voicemail.

If I could change anything at all about my life, it would be to go back to that moment and pick up the phone, to answer it and hear her voice on the other end. The fact that I didn't, the fact that I preferred to nurse my hurt instead of answering the call, will haunt me forever.

I don't expect sympathy for this. A mother should never ignore her own child. A mother should know better than to shatter into fragments when that child tells her she hates her. A mother should be able to track and chart the changing patterns of her daughter's mind and, even if she doesn't understand them, love them anyway. A mother should know to be better than her own fears and rages.

But it turned out that I knew none of these things then, and the next phone call I got, an hour later, was from the county police department, to tell me that there had been an accident—a teen driver, not looking at a busy intersection—and that someone identified as Eleanor Song-Morgan, age sixteen, had died in the impact. I was convinced that it was a cruel joke at first. I couldn't fathom how unlucky one person would have to be, to lose two parents and a daughter in the same way. "I must have done something really bad," I kept telling Dan in the weeks afterward. I was sedated most of that time, I think. "I must really deserve to be punished."

"Don't talk that way, Andy," he said, his eyes so full of love and pain I couldn't bear to look at him. His tears disgusted me. I found myself unable to cry, my eyes dry and burning in their sockets. Even when I sobbed, I could only scream until my throat felt shredded, without the cooling relief of tears. I imagined peeling back the layers of my flesh with my own hands, becoming nothing but bones, kindling. I was arid land, cursed. I wanted to set myself on fire, and the only thing that kept me from doing so was the medication, which made me so tired all I could do was sleep.

Elly would be twenty-two now. Old enough to be out of school, to be living on her own, had she wanted that. We would have become friends again, I think. In an alternate universe, perhaps we are sitting together in her new apartment, talking about TV shows, her job, Dan's foibles.

Lapsi gave me a chance to see Elly again at age five, when she had been at her sweetest. Almost more than missing her, I had wanted to divine where I had gone wrong with her back then. Had I been too strict, or too permissive? Had I been enough? Had I been too much? I felt sure, upon watching the introductory videos and pamphlets from Lapsi, and upon going through our photos and videos of her from that age to send on to their technicians, that I would somehow be able to map the coordinates of my grief and failings as a mother by seeing her as a child again.

"Are you sure that this is what you want?" our case counselor had asked upon reviewing our paperwork. "Most families opt to have their Lapsi calibrated to the most recent age of the deceased." She was smiling, but the lift of her eyebrows betrayed just a hint of judgment.

"Yes," I had said, squeezing Dan's hand. "Yes," I said again, making my voice level. "We're sure."

As the days went on, we gradually became used to Elly's presence. I grew less wary around her, and sometimes I even found myself thinking that she had actually come back to us, in some magical way, rather than the one afforded to us by technology. When we went outside, we walked with Elly between us, and I took pleasure in the sight of our three shadows on the ground. The happiness I had once felt, in the early years of Elly's life, did not come back, but it was replaced by something akin to peace. A satisfying slowness crept into our days, the routine of our lives threaded by the fact that this new Elly wanted only to be around us, to soak up the raw data generated by our conversations and interactions with her. She grew more Elly-like every day, but without a hint of the vitriol or temper that had made Elly so challenging later on, as though Lapsi had enhanced only her sweetest and best qualities. This Elly did not even throw tantrums.

We took her to the beach. The water was much too cold for swimming, but the sun was high in the sky, and for once there weren't too many people around. We unfurled a blanket, unpacked our sandwiches, and enjoyed the breeze off the water.

I took Elly to the water's edge and showed her the seashells that had washed up onshore. The wet sand looked as smooth as silk against the shoreline, and she shrieked with laughter at the sight of crabs scuttling past and seagulls diving for fish. Although I knew that she had simply been programmed to mimic Elly's capacity for joy, I laughed with her.

She let go of my hand and waded in, impervious to the chill of the waves. I hesitated for only a second before plunging in after her. Robot or no, she was light enough to be carried away by the current—only ten pounds heavier than the real Elly had been, because of the hardware. I stayed close beside her, wincing at the cold.

"Umma," Elly said. "Look." A small pale fish danced around our ankles, before darting away.

I marveled at her while she stared into the gray-green waters. Lapsi's technology had promised something akin to consciousness, the possibility of regeneration. I imagined the years of delicate and backbreaking work that someone—many someones—must have put into creating this Elly. The hands that had helped develop the hardware that made her possible, made her, in fact, sturdier and more durable than any real child.

"Do you remember when I told you about the haenyo, Elly?" I asked.

She nodded. "I'm going to be one when I get older," she said. "I'll get fishes for you and Daddy."

When I get older. She had said it so confidently. Not for the first time, I wondered if what we had done was cruel, to create a new life (of a kind) that could never change or age. This Elly and the real Elly had that in common, I realized—they would never grow up.

Lapsi had gotten it wrong. There was no possibility of life continuing after death. But that didn't mean the end of love, even if it was the kind of love that was easy. The kind of love that didn't demand anything of me, or require me to change, to become better, or to dive into the dark waters of my own faults and weaknesses and emerge with treasure. Elly would always be small and sweet and easy to love, never asking anything of me that I couldn't give.

The sun glinted in my eyes, and I could hear the gulls shrieking in the distance. "Let's go back in," I said.

The Arrow

It starts like this: You, staring at the stick balanced precariously on the edge of your bathroom sink and praying, *Please God, I'll do anything,* but you can't think of what to say after that, what to offer that might be a fair trade for not being pregnant. When the pink cross appears, it feels like a confirmation of what you've known all along—that God, if he exists, does not give a shit.

But once your initial panic subsides and you've managed to catch your breath, you begin to feel tender toward it, this un-asked-for clump of new cells that seems so determined to live. You find that you sleep better at night, comforted by the presence taking root in your body, unfurling itself one piece of genetic information at a time. You buy yourself fresh fruit and vegetables at the market. You take vitamins. You hold yourself more carefully on the subway.

This is ridiculous, you think, but instead of making a decision, you go looking for signs. You decide you'll start believing in anything, just to get some kind of guidance on what to do about the baby. You pay an astrologer in Bushwick two hundred dollars to squint at a computer printout that has your date, time, and place of birth stamped on it in smeared DeskJet ink, even though your time of birth is just a guess you hazarded because you didn't want to call and ask your mother, who raised you all by herself in your father's absence and has never let you forget it. The astrologer, a girl a few years younger than you who has one pierced eyebrow and goes by Citrine, a name she's clearly picked for herself, tells you that you have a strong propensity toward self-sabotage. That your fire moon and water sun are conspiring against each other. When you ask her about babies, she says that motherhood won't come naturally to you, but that you're destined to raise three strong boys at some point in your future, which sounds depressing and inaccurate.

You go to an ayahuasca ceremony with your friend Melissa at someone's apartment in Gowanus, a huge one-bedroom with bumpy white walls and flickering candles everywhere, and, at the last minute, decide not to drink the tea offered to you. You sit back and watch, feeling embarrassed when Melissa starts to channel a spirit that makes her sob and call out for her mother. On the subway ride back home, you see an old Asian woman wearing plastic bags on her feet asleep on the seat across from you, her purse agape. Before you get off the train, you tuck a ten-dollar bill inside her purse and zip its mouth closed. She does not really look like your mother, but these days, any Asian woman over the age of sixty looks like your mother to you.

You go to church for the first time in years. You avoid making eye contact with anyone who nods or smiles in your direction, and practically flee at the conclusion of the service. You come back, not during the afternoon service for twenty-to-forty-somethings, but to the sparsely attended early-morning service, where it's mostly older people. You screw your eyes shut and try to picture God—not as the bearded white man in the clouds that you imagined scowling at your pee stick just before it went positive, but as a warm, healing ball of divine light and energy that Melissa told you she saw once during an acid trip out in the Arizona desert. But all you see are bursts of color in the dark behind your eyelids. You remember how, as a child, you used to mash the heels of your hands into your closed eyelids to make colors appear in that dark. How, whenever your mother hit you with the back of her hand, you could close your eyes and conjure those blossoms of light in your mind, like fireworks seen through a dirty window, or anemones in dark water.

When you open your eyes all you see are the backs of old people's heads, nodding in their separate pews, and the spit flecks flying from the pastor's mouth.

Here are the facts: You are not in any way ready to have a baby, living paycheck to paycheck in an apartment you cannot afford, in a city that feels increasingly unfamiliar to you.

But everywhere you turn, the world seems ready to convince you otherwise. The neighbors who move into the unit across from yours, a small family—a wife, a husband, and their two children, all four of them red-cheeked and thick-limbed and smiley—make your teeth ache with loneliness. You listen to the patter of their children's footsteps and the babble of their high baby voices and wonder if they are happy. The father is friendly and the mother avoids you, her eyes rarely meeting yours when you stop to hold the door open for her and the multiple tote bags she is always carrying. She always seems tired, and her fatigue feels like a rebuke to yours—you, who have so few responsibilities or obligations to anyone and fulfill them so badly.

Here are some more facts: You are pregnant and you do not know exactly who the father is, because, in the span of one bad week, you slept with your ex, a chef whose late hours you still haven't unlearned; your married coworker who says he and his wife are experimenting with ethical nonmonogamy; and a tattoo artist you met in a cheesy bar in Williamsburg. This all took place in the days after you called home for the first time in a year to wish your mother a happy birthday and she hung up on you.

Sleeping with your ex was easy enough, like climbing back onto a bike after falling off. After you finished most of a bottle of peach-flavored soju, doing plasticky shots alone in your dusty kitchen, you called him at two in the morning, when you knew he'd be buzzed off Cognac and cigarettes and just getting off work. He came over with a Styrofoam container of miso-honey-chili-brined chicken wings, and you licked the sweet-salty glaze off each other's fingers and gnawed all the bones clean. He always liked that you were an eater, didn't care if your stomach protruded after a good meal or that the upper sections of your arms had grown soft and fleshy in the months since you'd left each other. Afterward, he fucked you on your secondhand couch. The floorboards creaked and the couch springs screamed, and you worried that the family next door might hear, until you did not care anymore. In the morning he was gone, without even leaving so much as a stray hair on the couch cushions, and then you threw up peach-flavored chunks in the bathroom until your body felt as light and hollow as the discarded chicken bones at the bottom of your trash can.

Your coworker you fucked in the women's bathroom at work, long after everyone else had gone home. He made small, grateful sounds as he moved in and out of you, which made you feel so generous you let him finish inside you, telling him that you were on the pill, even though you are negligent about taking your doses at the same time each day. "Megan hasn't let me do that in ages," he said, his damp mouth pressed to your neck, and you wanted to shake him off, annoyed at the mention of his wife, a woman you've met once or twice at office holiday parties. You remember her being tall, pink-skinned, and honey-haired, with freckles and an athletic glow about her. You wonder if he has ever tried to count all the freckles on her face and shoulders, or played connect-the-dots on them with his tongue. You don't want to feel guilty about Megan, but you do.

You went home with the tattoo artist after he let you win at darts at a bar, and because he had an appealingly crooked smile, one gold tooth flashing in the back of his mouth like a star. In his dimly lit apartment, the walls washed with red neon from the gas-station sign outside, you traced the lines of his tattoos with your fingers, the teeth and talons and feathers and leaves inked all over his arms and chest, and he told you how much each one hurt; how the pain eventually starts feeling so intense you can get high from it; how afterward, for a few hours, colors seem brighter and everything is louder. Before you left, he said you should call him if you ever wanted to get the tattoo idea you'd told him about, a slim arrow pointing down the length of your forearm.

"Where is it supposed to be pointing?" he'd asked, and you had hesitated before answering.

For much of your life, you had been driven toward success, because that was the only surefire way to get out from under your mother. In school, you learned that sharks die if they don't keep moving, and you had followed the same principle, applying for scholarship after scholarship and working as many side jobs as you could fit into your schedule, all in the name of leaving your small, smog-choked Southern California town behind. You thought of your fear as a golden arrow that pointed outward from the dark surrounding your mother's house, a beam that led you away from orange smoke and bumper-to-bumper traffic on the freeway and endless sunshine and rotting fruit on sidewalks, toward a future where you were no one's daughter, where the only dreams and desires you had to follow were your own.

Whenever you call home, your mother berates you for leaving her, for not coming to visit, in the same breath in which she starts accusing you of stealing from her—her money, her youth, her life. She tells you that God is watching you, that he knows what you are up to. When you hang up, your hands are shaking, and you have to stay drunk for several days.

But this is all too much to tell a one-time hookup, and so you lie and tell him that the arrow represents your zodiac sign, and he tells you that he has the same one, isn't that funny?

You wonder what sign this baby will be born under. If it is born. You do the math in your head, decide it'll be a summer baby. "Summer is the worst time to have a child," your mother always said, as though you yourself were not born in the middle of July.

This is what your friends say: that you are crazy for even thinking about having it. All of them make more money than you, their arrows pointing them toward bigger and better and more expensive futures than yours. Diana and her girlfriend are saving up for in vitro. Sujin wants to have two kids and move to Long Island but is waiting to make partner at her law firm before she starts trying with Andy. Melissa is engaged to a software engineer who goes to Burning Man with her every year.

You are sure that all of them talk about you behind your back in hushed, pitying tones—your primarily administrative job at a glorified online content farm that, despite your hope that it would turn into an editing position, has remained a dead end;

your bad taste in men; your tendency to drink just a little too much. Their voices practically vibrate with pleasurable anticipation at brunch or happy hour when they ask you to tell them about your latest escapades. "We're living vicariously through you," they say, sighing. "We're such old ladies these days."

The thing no one tells you about living in New York City is that it's all fun and free shots at 3:00 p.m. and parties at someone's boyfriend's loft in TriBeCa at 10:00 p.m. and sloppy slices of pizza at 2:00 a.m. and cab rides home at 4:00 a.m., until it is not, and then the engagements and promotions and movings-away start, and the music stops, and you are the only one left without a chair. *When did parties start ending so early?* you wonder while climbing in and out of the gray train of your life. Even the rats that scurry along the subway tracks look tired. Maybe they, too, dream of life in an easier town, with a yard and a house and a better public-school system.

Sometimes you dream of picking up and moving to another place entirely, a remote desert town or a cabin in the woods, without telling anyone. Because you're beginning to worry that you will never change, that you'll continue sleeping with the wrong people and drinking too much, until your mistakes outgrow the lessons you've tried to glean from them and you become exactly what your mother always said you were—a mistake. A failure.

You are both alarmed by and resentful of the passage of time, the years that have come and gone without making you into a better, more successful person, a kinder, more forgiving daughter. There is a part of you that wants to have this baby because you think becoming a mother will pull you toward that imagined version of yourself, will make your arrow burn gold again.

The internet tells you that at this stage the baby is the size of a raspberry. You toy with the idea of making an appointment at a clinic you happen to pass every day on the way to work, but you cannot bring yourself to pick up the phone and call.

You linger by the baby clothes in Target. You hold a pair of impossibly tiny pink sneakers in the palm of your hand, touch lavender and yellow tulle skirts. For some reason, you feel absolutely certain that the baby is a girl.

A clerk smiles at you and asks how far along you are. "Two months," you say, startled.

"I can always tell," the woman says. "Congratulations."

You want to ask her what she thinks you should do, but you just smile back, pretending that you are a woman whose pregnancy has been planned, who is safe and loved.

You finally break down and call your mother, your Korean even clunkier than usual. There is a silence, and for a moment you think she's hung up, and then she asks you to repeat yourself.

"I'm pregnant, Umma," you say. You are so terrified that, for a moment, all thirty-five years of your life flash before your eyes. You brace yourself for screaming, for the sound of her smashing the phone into the wall, the way she did when you told her you were dropping out of law school years ago.

But, instead, your mother just asks you how far along you are. If you are eating well. And then, hesitantly, who the father is.

"He's married," you say. A half-truth, or at least one-third of it. "He doesn't know."

"Are you going to tell him?" she asks.

"I don't know," you say, and she sighs, not in the way of a mother exasperated or angry with her child, but in the way of a woman who knows how these things work, because she went through the same thing with your father, when she had you.

When she calls the next day to tell you that she is flying out to

New York, you are relieved that you will no longer be alone in all this, until the fear sets in.

At the airport, she is thinner than you remember her being. She is dressed in a performance fleece and wrinkled pants with a floral print. Her hair has been dyed a brassy red-brown that makes her face look even paler than usual. When you were growing up, she hated how dark your skin got in the summertime— "Just like your father," she'd say—and would chase you around with long-sleeved shirts and wide-brimmed plastic visors. At fifteen, you learned to eschew sunblock at the beach in an effort to achieve a golden tan, just like your best friend Mimi Kang's, whose parents could afford to send her to tennis camp in the summer, but you only succeeded in getting your first sunburn. And even though you know better now and you wear SPF every day, whenever you look in the mirror, you can hear your mother bemoaning your stupidity, the premature wrinkles she predicted would follow your repeated exposures to the sun.

You pull her into a stiff hug, noticing how terribly light she feels in your arms. She is full of complaints about the flight, the weather, the other passengers, how dirty New York is. She has only brought one carry-on item with her, a suitcase with a half-broken handle and a squeaky wheel, which you end up pulling through the terminal.

She hates your apartment, is horrified by what she calls "the state of it," even though you've been cleaning for days. But you realize this is a good thing, because it gives her something to fuss about. Within an hour of her arrival, she is on her hands and knees, scrubbing your kitchen floor with a vigor that you would not expect of a sixty-four-year-old. You squint at the rubber gloves she is wearing, which you are almost 100 percent sure you do not own. Could she have brought them with her?

"I didn't raise you to be dirty like this," she says as she scours your stovetop, which is crusted with grease streaks and blackened crumbs. You don't have the heart to tell her that the apartment was like this when you moved in, that you barely cook anyway. Instead, you go to your room and lie down to sleep—you've been so tired recently—and when you wake up, nearly two hours later, the whole apartment smells like seaweed soup. Your mother spoons a mound of white rice onto a plate and pushes a bowl of soup at you. Golden pools of oil gleam on its surface. "It's good for the baby," she says.

In the mornings, your mother wakes up before you do and makes barley tea. She sends you off to work with a thermos of it. "No coffee," she says. "It's bad for the baby." Beyond this, and the fact that she buys you prenatal vitamins along with clusters of citrus fruits that she insists are good for the baby, you and your mother do not discuss your pregnancy much. You study the fruit piled on your kitchen table. When the morning light filters through your windows, the orange and yellow globes smell sun-warmed and ripe, like a small orchard is growing in your apartment.

There is no question in your mind, now that she is here, that you will keep this baby. Because your mother, no matter how you feel about her, is a reminder that what you want—to have this baby and raise it on your own—is possible.

Your married coworker texts you during the workday, asking if you'd like to go out sometime this week, on what he calls "a proper date." He says Megan is cool with it. You feel a great weariness sandbag your bones. You tell him a version of the truth, that you are not feeling well and that your mother is staying with you for a few weeks. He expresses his sympathy, before asking you to send him a dirty pic. You oblige, because who knows when you will be desired again. You go into the bathroom and contort yourself over the toilet bowl to get the shot, in the stall next to the one you fucked him in.

You wonder how long you will be able to keep your pregnancy hidden at work. If you'll need, eventually, to get some kind of paternity test.

Your friends do not understand any of this. "I thought you and your mom didn't speak," they say. "You told us she was awful to you growing up." You don't deny this, the times she locked you out of the house for talking back or coming home from school with liquor on your breath—although you never got in trouble for your grades; you never let those slip, no matter how much you wanted to die on a day-to-day basis.

Once, you unfolded a paper clip and etched line after line of red down your forearms, just to feel something. When your mother saw the cuts, the jagged borders where you had dug into your skin again and again, all she said was "If you're going to do it, do it right. And kill me, too, while you're at it."

Later, you told yourself that this was her way of trying to get you to stop. That she was a scared single mother working two jobs to support you and herself and didn't have the slightest clue of what to do with you, her angry, unruly teenage daughter. That she was using reverse psychology, Jedi mind-tricking you, in the way of all Korean mothers. And it had worked, because the pit of chalky despair you felt in your stomach every morning turned into an ironclad resignation to keep on living, just to spite her.

But how can you explain to your friends that this mother, the one in your apartment now, seems to be a distant cousin to the one you remember from childhood? That, though she is still as sharp-tongued as ever, she has grown softer around the edges? During the day, when you are at work, sending fake-chipper emails and avoiding walking by your married coworker's cubicle, your mother has apparently taken to walking in the park. She does a full loop, she tells you proudly, and even though she remains disgusted with the general grime of the city and disapproves of the fact that Americans do not pick up thoroughly after their too-large dogs, she likes the park, its graceful trees and rolling hills and winding pathways.

At dinner, over the dishes of your childhood, she tells you about little things she saw that day. A bouquet of yellow roses, abandoned on a curb. A single swan, floating on the green surface of a pond in the park. A kite shaped like an octopus, with eight legs streaming behind its bulbous painted head, and a child in a red jacket attached to it, laughing whenever the wind blew the octopus farther upward. Her voice is soft and wistful, and you recall that, before the smog of Los Angeles, before the glittering skyline of Seoul, where she met your father while working as an office girl at his company, she had grown up in a village to the north, in the mountains, where pine trees grew tall and mornings were blue and misty.

The image of the kite reminds you of one of the few times you met your father. He was a tall, dignified man, handsome, you suppose, judging by the one photo you have of him. He was married when he met your mother, and he is still married to his wife ("that woman," your mother calls her). Your mother had been your father's mistress, which was why he did not live with you, why he only came to see you on certain days of the year, and why your presents from him were always expensive and slightly wrong, like they had been purchased for another child. Like the heavy wooden chess set you never learned how to play, or the set of leather-bound encyclopedias you were too embarrassed to tell him no one used anymore.

Only once had he ever brought you a present you loved. It was a stuffed plush octopus that could also be worn as a hat, with

Velcro attached to its legs. You named her Olivia and carried her around everywhere, until her pink plush turned a dull gray. When your father stopped visiting and answering your mother's calls, she threw out the presents he had given you, including the encyclopedias—all except for Olivia, whom you wedged into a hidden spot between your mattress and bed frame, although you eventually lost track of her, too.

You show your mother the ultrasound, and the two of you admire the dark shimmer of the baby's heartbeat, tiny but strong. Your mother's eyes swim. She takes the ultrasound from you, sits with it. "Your father didn't go with me to my appointments after I found out you'd be a girl," she said. "I always thought if you had been a son he would have stayed in the end."

Even though it's what you've always suspected—that your mother had hated you for not being enough to keep your father around—it still hurts to hear her say it. "Maybe not," you say. "Maybe he was just an asshole."

You learn that the baby is now the size of a plum, that she is growing fingernails, and that a fine layer of hair covers her now, like a carpet. How clever the engine of the human body is, you think to yourself as you stare at the emerging bump, the rise and slope of your stomach.

A few weeks later, you tell your ex, your married coworker, the tattoo artist. One by one, they panic, pace, and finally calm down when you reassure them that you don't expect anything of them, that this is your decision and that you will be doing this on your own. Your ex says "Shit," and opens a bottle of whiskey. Your married coworker cries. The tattoo artist asks if he can touch your stomach, and you say no.

You realize that you are living the plot of a romantic comedy, except that no one is laughing and the only romance here is the one developing between your mother and the baby. Even though you've read online that it's still too early to feel the baby's movements, you can't help but think you feel them—joyful and quick, like those of a sea otter cavorting in the waves. She seems particularly active whenever she hears your mother's voice, as though she, too, wants to participate in the conversation.

Pregnancy makes your dreams vivid, eerie. You dream that your body has turned to water, that the baby has somehow floated out of you in your sleep and is lying, nestled and flippered, in the twin rivers of your arms. She has slippery skin like a dolphin's, but she is perfect. You dream that you are standing in a dark field and a golden star spills from the sky, its tail a fiery stream that fans out into the shape of an arrow. You follow it until you wake up.

Your mother has started referring to the two of you as one entity, referred to simply as "the baby." As in, "The baby needs to eat," or "And how is the baby feeling today?" She is happier than you've ever known her, singing hymns in the morning when you wake up and making elaborate meals for the three of you. If you had known that all it would take was getting pregnant to get your mother to love you, you would have done it ages ago, you think.

Your hair, which has been pin-straight for most of your life, starts to go wavy. Your chanmori, baby hairs, get caught in the static electricity generated by the friction of your wool scarf against your cheek. "It's hormones," your mother says. "When I was pregnant with you, my left foot grew half a shoe size. I still can't wear heels." You feel as though you should apologize for this, but you don't, because for once it doesn't sound like your mother is blaming you for ruining her life. In fact, she sounds almost dreamy, nostalgic.

You take your mother shopping for a winter coat, because she has never had occasion to buy one, after more than thirty years in Southern California. Together, you linger in brightly lit aisles, murmuring over merchandise. You hold up coats to her thin frame in the mirrors, like she used to do to you at the Salvation Army, where you got all your clothes as a child.

She selects a purple coat with gray faux-fur trim, a far cry from the sober navy or practical black coats you thought she might choose. "I didn't know you liked purple," you say.

"There's a lot of things you don't know about me," she says.

Outside, the city is dressed in red and green. A small, light-up Christmas tree in a store window shudders colorful sparks. Your mother wears her coat out of the store and links arms with you. You realize that a stranger pausing to observe the two of you would think you were any ordinary mother and daughter, rather than two people who just happen to be related to each other, women linked by their carelessness with men, the loneliness of their lives made legible in the way they lean on each other but do not speak or laugh or even turn to look at each other. The baby dances inside you, performing a quick shuffle, and you zip up your coat against the knife's edge of the wind. *Things will be different for you,* you tell her.

A neon rose blinks in a window. AURA READINGS, a sign says. You pull your mother inside, emboldened by the success of the coat. "I've read about this place online," you tell her.

Inside, you take turns sitting in front of a large black camera. A bored-looking man in a tan blazer explains the process to you, and you translate for your mother. The camera takes a long exposure of the subject, he says, while tiny rainbow crystals inside the device, activated by light, can determine, via photo capture, what color a person's aura is.

Your aura is a soft cloud of yellow and green. "Yellow is good," the man says authoritatively. "It means confidence. Green means renewal and energy. You carry within you a strength and resolve for the future."

"That's the baby," your mother says proudly.

Your mother's aura is bluish, a moody billow of violet and indigo. "Purple signifies compassion," the young man says. "Blue means awareness. Sadness, mixed with wisdom and maturity."

Your mother nods slowly when you explain this to her, as though sadness is her birthright. You study her large eyes and high cheekbones, which you did not inherit; her large ears and thin eyebrows, which you did. The small mole at the corner of her mouth, which you used to stare at as a kid in order to avoid crying whenever she yelled at you, because crying would only make the yelling worse. "You think you've done something good?" she would say at the first sign of tears. "You think you deserve to cry?"

"What?" your mother says.

"I was just thinking about how much we don't look alike," you say.

"Nonsense," your mother says, looking at your two aura pictures side by side. She taps the image of your face. "Maybe when you were little. But now you look just like me," she says. You bend over the photos to see what she sees, and maybe it's just a trick of the light, or because you want it to be so, but it turns out there is more than a passing similarity between your faces, in the way you both lift your eyes to the camera's gaze and your chins come to a determined point.

Here is how it ends: One morning you wake up and everything is wrong. It feels like a hand has reached inside you to wring your womb dry. You rush to the bathroom, and it is as you suspected; more blood than you'd ever thought possible crimsons your underwear, your pants. You close your eyes, wait to wake up, to feel the sea otter flutter inside you that will let you know all is right. But it doesn't come, and the animal wail that fills the air like a siren surprises you, and then your mother bursts into the bathroom, and you realize that the wails are coming from you.

You call in sick, stay in bed for what seems like years. Your baby, the magical fish that swam inside the bowl of you for nearly twelve weeks, is gone, like a balloon that has been released into the sky. From far away, you see your mother hover over you, urging you to eat. She pushes a bowl of rice at you, like you are a sick dog, and you push it away. Your arms ache. Your breasts ache. You collapse into yourself, until you turn into a story that's been told so many times it's no longer recognizable. She tells you that you have to go to the doctor, but you refuse.

"Go away," you tell her, in a fever of hate. "Go home. I don't need you here anymore." She retreats, for once, her face a dim moon above the rising tide of your rage, her mouth so down-turned it's almost comical, like a parody of sadness.

One morning, you wake up so early that it is still dark outside. You feel empty, like an eggshell that's lost the slip of its yolk. The apartment is silent, and you realize that, for the first time in a long while, you are alone. That your mother has finally left, and that perhaps this was God's way of answering your prayers after all, because hadn't you prayed to not be pregnant, in the beginning?

But when you stumble into your kitchen, your mother is there, standing over the stove and muttering to herself over a pot of juk, with just the stove light on for company.

"Finally, you're awake. You have to eat," she says.

You sit down, too weak to argue. A bowl of juk, topped with soy sauce and sesame oil and scallions, materializes in front of you. The handful of times your mother let you stay home sick from school while you were growing up, she would make this porridge for you. Someday, she'd say, I'll teach you how to make it for your own children.

She doesn't say anything, just sits down next to you and squeezes your left hand as you spoon juk into your mouth, crying all the while, until you can't eat anymore. Afterward, she smooths back the still-curly baby hairs from your face, with a gentleness you have never known before.

"I've booked my return ticket," she tells you, and you nod.

"Thank you," you say. "For staying."

She does not tell you that she loves you, nor does she tell you that everything is going to be okay, because both of you are past believing things like that. And as the sun climbs over the lip of the sky, and the two of you watch its ascent, gold filling the corners of your apartment, you begin to understand that there is only this moment, and then the next, and then the next, and that the only thing to do in the meantime is to keep on living.

Names for Fireflies

Stacy Shin tells me the only way to get my mosquito bites to stop itching is to spit on them and make an "X" across them with my nails. She wets my kneecap with her spit and then inscribes the edge of her thumbnail over the itchiest, reddest bite of all, the mark leaving a white imprint on my tan summer skin. Her foamy saliva makes the itching stop almost instantly.

It's the summer of 2002. I'm twelve years old, and so is Stacy. My mother takes me to the mall to buy a bra, which feels like a harness for something I didn't know I needed to keep in place.

I kiss Esther Cho's older brother, Joon, at a birthday party while wearing it and let him cup his hand around my breasts. Our teeth knock together like jumbled forks in a drawer, but it's not so bad, until he tells everyone, and the other boys corner me, their lips puckered up like goldfish. When I punch one of them, I'm the only one who gets in trouble, and my parents tell me that it's all my fault for kissing Joon in the first place. Then everyone stops talking to me except Stacy, who doesn't get invited to parties even though she's pretty and her family lives in a big, beautiful house, because she prays in the cafeteria at lunch, closing her eyes and moving her lips in front of everyone, like a freak. Only I don't think she's a freak at all. I want to poke Stacy in the ribs when she starts praying, tell her to open her eyes and stop calling so much attention to herself, but part of me also likes that she never seems to care that it makes everyone else whisper and giggle.

Stacy invites me over and teaches me how to do the butterfly in her pool, and we play lifeguard and practice saving each other. I watch the chlorinated water lap against her bony chest, her skin so pale it turns blue in the water. I want us to stay in the pool until our skin deepens to the color of the evening sky and we grow fins and gills, two blue fish-girls circling each other. At night, I pray to God to make Stacy like me like I like her.

Stacy and I stay outside until the sun gets low and the air gets thick with fireflies, which Stacy calls lightning bugs. I type "firefly" into the blinking search box on my computer screen and learn that there are over a dozen names for them, including "moon bug," which is the best one of all. Stacy and I catch one in a jar, but she tells me to let it go, because it looks lonely blinking on its own inside the glass. She unscrews the lid and it helicopters itself into the night, a spiral of gold as it moves first toward her face, then toward the stars.

Stacy's mother is pretty, just like her, but she always looks like she's been crying, and her father is almost always on the phone, with the door to his office shut. I come home from Stacy's house with monogrammed gift bags filled with thick skin creams, fine lotions, and pearly lipsticks that Stacy's mom has too much of, and when my mother sees them, she clucks her tongue at the extravagance, but she doesn't send them back. We stack them in the bathroom cabinet, and sometimes I open the vials and jars and tubes and breathe deep, pretending I'm back at Stacy's house.

Sunday afternoons, after church, Stacy's family and mine eat at the Chinese buffet restaurant in Paramus. We eat strategically, starting with the lo mein before proceeding to the fried chicken wings, egg rolls, and steamed dumplings, and then getting soft-serve ice cream and bowls of red Jell-O for dessert. I like watching Stacy eat, her lips glistening with fat as she tears at another chicken leg.

We flip over the oil-stained paper placemats and play MASH on them with our fathers' ballpoint pens, divining our futures. Mansion, Apartment, Shack, House. Three children, two children, seven children, none. After dinner, we crack open our fortune cookies and read the slips of paper inside to each other—*You will receive good news; If you are always going around looking for trouble, you will soon find it*—before swallowing them, the thin paper melting on our tongues like sugar. While our parents argue over who gets to pay the check, Stacy and I sneak handfuls of sprinkles from the dessert bar, until there is a small radius of pink and yellow and green confetti around our chairs, and our tongues are patchworked with food dye. We ignore how frantic the arguments over the bill can get, how Stacy's mother clutches her father's arm and whispers, loud enough for the whole table to hear, how he needs to stop showing off, to yangbo, or yield, for once in his life. "Don't talk to me that way, you person," he says, in a way that I can't tell whether it's a joke or not, and on the way home, my mother says to my father, "I guess it's true that money can't buy everything."

One Sunday morning, Stacy and I are sitting next to each other in church when I send God a hello, just to see if He's listening. It's as I suspected: nothing. I try to pay attention to the sermon, but I get bored and pretend I am on the ceiling as a small iridescent fly with a thousand lenses in each of my disked, amber eyes. Stacy cries during the prayer, which I know because I'm watching her from the corner of my many-lensed eyes, even though I'm supposed to keep them closed. Her lashes are so long they cast shadows across her wet cheekbones.

"Sometimes I feel God all around me," she says later. "Don't you?" We're sitting in her dad's car, eating soggy French fries from the Wendy's nearby. I want to tell her yes, but I don't know how to say that I don't think God is real, at least not like He is for her.

Our pastor is always talking about fire—tongues of flame licking the heads of true believers, lakes of fire filled with sinners. When I close my eyes and try to imagine God, I don't see any of those fires. I want to tell Stacy that instead, I see the orbs of a million fireflies, lightning bugs, glow flies, golden sparklers, moon bugs, lighting up a dark night, but I don't.

Two Sundays from now, Stacy and her mother will move away without telling anyone else, because, as my mother tells me later, her parents are getting a divorce. When I ask her why that means Stacy had to leave, she tells me to shush and stop asking questions about things I don't understand. Three months from now, Stacy's house will be up for sale, with a sign out front featuring a realtor's smiling face, and the pool will be drained and covered up, and the white family that eventually moves in will almost never use it.

But I don't know all that yet. I still think Stacy and I will always have each other, that we have so much time.

I don't tell Stacy that when she spit on my knees all I could think about was how her spit might taste. Or that when I wet the bites on my body with my mouth, I imagined that I was kissing her, breathing into her after pulling her out of deep-blue water. That I think maybe God is just whatever good news is waiting for us, and the trouble that always finds us. Or maybe God is the warm spit from her mouth cocooning my bites, soothing whatever it is that makes me want to tear open my skin again and again. Or that maybe God can be whatever we want to believe, and that I'd rather believe in her wet-lashed shadows, her dappled tongue, the imprint of her nails on my skin, than anything else in the world.

Honey and Sun

We were born—two minutes apart, identical but for a blush-colored diamond that appeared on one of our right shoulder blades, and not on the other's—into a world of beauty and weight. The objects in our home were heavy and had a forbidding sheen, and many were much, much older than us. We were not allowed to touch most of them, because we were inclined to destroy things, often knocking over vases, staining brocade cushions, or inadvertently smashing dinner plates. We buried the evidence in our backyard, one of us keeping watch while the other clawed at the dirt with her small fingers.

We imagined that someday, hundreds of years from now, these buried remnants—the shards of porcelain and china, the fine fabrics we had spilled juice on, the smashed tubes of Mother's coral and mauve lipsticks—would sprout roots that tendriled through the soil to form an underground version of our house. Two little underground girls would live there too, just like us, but with a mother made of earth and a father made of rainwater. We envied them, these shadow versions of ourselves with no eyes or mouths, but with root hands and root arms that stretched on and on for miles, interlinked forever.

Our real mother was like a hummingbird—tiny and beautiful, never alighting too long on any one thing. She rarely ate, living on a diet of boiled rice and black coffee, and she wrapped her tiny waist with a long tape measure every morning. When we were very young, she used to measure us too, and we'd laugh as she wrapped the tape around our foreheads or our chubby arms and legs. She wore long, full-skirted dresses and heavy bracelets, which seemed to be the only things tethering her to the earth. Without them, we thought, she would rise up into the sky like a soap bubble.

Mother cried often and easily over our many failings. She bemoaned our inability to keep still or clean, our insistence on refusing things in unison. Especially, our lack of interest in the clothes she bought us—pastel dresses as confining as small suits of armor, and shiny shoes that pinched our toes. We wanted to be free to climb trees, jump into puddles, spin in circles until the world became streaks of color and we had to lie down to watch the streaks slow to a dizzying stop.

"No one likes dirty little girls," Mother said when we tracked mud into the hallway.

"Little girls shouldn't eat like starving wolves," when we bolted our food at the dinner table.

"Don't you girls want to look pretty?" when we eschewed the beribboned, apple-green dresses she had picked out for us.

We consulted each other: We were not good, pretty, or clean. Was this a problem? After some deliberation, we decided that it wasn't. We didn't mind how the other children at our school whispered about us. We didn't mind when Lindsay Twixby raised her hand and complained about sitting next to us because she said we smelled; we liked the way we smelled, like sun-bake and damp earth. We told each other we didn't mind when we were passed over for birthday parties or trips to the movies. Our teachers wrote notes to our parents—"Is everything okay at home?"— but they stopped when they learned the notes only resulted in weepy phone calls from Mother, who always got nervous around other adults, as if she thought she wasn't one of them.

If our mother was a hummingbird, our father was the sun. He was everywhere and nowhere, his presence felt in every corner of our house. Most mothers we knew or saw on TV seemed to barely tolerate their husbands, often rolling their eyes at them or shrugging off kisses, but Mother glittered whenever Father was around. He smelled of cool water and leather. He had a handsome, angular face and eyes like a camera lens—narrowing when he smiled, focusing only on you. He had a demanding, complicated job we did not understand that involved long trips away and hushed phone conversations behind closed doors. During his absences, Mother ate even less and buzzed around buying things that would make the house feel fuller without him. He left our home sunless for months at a time before reappearing with little notice at random, festive intervals, his pockets filled with expensive new toys that always broke after a week or two.

Our dolls, Cardamom and Sage, were the only toys he ever brought home that lasted. He had gone on another trip and returned with two cloth dolls, one in a red pinafore and the other in a blue one. He said, "They're sisters, just like you."

We eyed them skeptically. They were not even the kind of dolls who could sit up on their own, or pee. They had buttons for eyes and red thread for lips. We would have put them away along with the rest of our abandoned toys had it not been for Cardamom, the red-pinafore doll, who said, after we had finished reading aloud to each other that night, "What happened next?"

She told us, "I'm Cardamom. This is Sage." Sage stood up and gave a bow so deep she toppled over. And after that, we couldn't get them to shut up.

Cardamom was loud and opinionated. She would announce to the room, apropos of nothing, "Homework is stupid," or "I hate broccoli." Sage was full of spare advice and untruths that we loved. She bent over one of our drawings and asked, "Would a house really only have two windows? Most have at least sixteen."

"Let's break things and cause mayhem," Cardamom suggested once. "Let's eat only strawberries and cream and howl at the moon." Sage said, "The moon is made entirely of a fine blend of Gouda and Edam. Howling at her is permissible only during the month of October, when it is her birthday."

The dolls slept between us at night, pretending to breathe in sync with us. Sometimes they braided our hair into one joined rope so we could stagger around like one monstrous, four-legged beast. And when we cried at night, lonely for reasons we did not understand, they wiped away our tears with their soft cotton hands. It was enough, we thought, to have each other, to have the trees and the puddles and our underground house and the dolls, even when other kids were mean and our mother was a hummingbird and our father was a sun that never stayed.

In the spring of our eleventh year, strange women began calling the house and hanging up whenever Mother answered. "Hello? Hello?" Mother said into the receiver, sounding like a lost parrot.

One day, when we picked up the phone, the woman on the other end said, in a smoky, velvet voice, "How old are you, honey? Is your father there?"

"We're not your honey," we said.

The woman laughed and was about to say something else when our mother called from the other room, "Who is it?" The woman hung up.

That night, we heard shouts and fighting coming from our parents' bedroom. Cardamom and Sage woke us, scared by the noises, and we four huddled together with our ears pressed against our bedroom door.

We heard Mother wail, "Is she prettier than me?" There was the sound of something expensive shattering, and then the sound of our father's footsteps down the stairs. The slam of the front gate, his car driving away.

Mother took to her bed, her sobs occasionally leaking out from beneath the door in murky pools. We waited for Father to come back, to bring light and color back to our house the way he always had before, but he did not, and the calls from the strange women stopped.

The fabrics and fragments and lipsticks we had buried in our backyard began to resurface, growing into elegant, woman-shaped orchids that emitted heavy clouds of fragrance. The smell gave us bad dreams, so we yanked the orchids out of the earth and ate the roots; the bitter soil turned to mud inside our mouths. The dolls showed us how to boil the roots in water and add salt for flavor, salt we later sprinkled on the ground to keep the flowers from growing. But the orchids came back, again and again, their scent thickening the air and troubling our sleep.

A few weeks later, our uncle came for a visit from Korea. We were digging more holes in our backyard when he arrived. "Come say hello," Mother said to us, trying to smile.

We bowed stiffly, inclining our heads. Uncle had a silvery

beard and moved and spoke slowly, like a wizened tree come to life. His face rarely moved, and his eyes were lined by time, even though he was only six years older than Mother.

He offered us chalky ginseng candy from his pockets. "You're doing well in school? And listening to your mother?" His eyes searched ours, as though the answers to his questions were written on our faces.

"Not really," we mumbled around the candy, looking at the floor. Cardamom and Sage cleared their throats, waiting to be introduced, but we kept them hidden behind us.

Uncle asked, "Don't you have anything else to say for yourselves?" and we said, "We don't speak Korean too great."

Uncle told Mother that children should know how to speak the language of their parents. He asked why we were so dirty. Our eyes swiveled from him to Mother as they talked, then back again; our hair was tangled and matted and our teeth were black from eating soil. Mother's eyes filled with easy tears. "You can't imagine how hard it is, trying to get them to listen to anything I say."

Uncle caught sight of Cardamom eavesdropping. "Aren't they too old to be playing with dolls?" he said. He reached for Cardamom, and her face became still, a stopped clock.

We told him not to touch her. Mother was horrified. "Apologize at once," she said.

Uncle's laughter reminded us of heavy, distant footsteps walking down a long hallway. "It's clear they take after their father," he said.

It was decided that Mother needed a break. She said we would stay with Uncle in Korea, and sent us off with our suitcases and kisses that dissolved immediately on our foreheads. We noticed she had packed a bag herself, and she was wearing makeup again, a palette of colors that seemed too loud for her small, pale face.

"Where will you go?" we asked her.

She said, "I need to find the pieces of myself and put them back together again." She sounded like one of the books that lay around her bedroom, the ones with sunsets or flowers on the covers and titles like *Your Best You Now*.

We turned around in the cab on the way to the airport to wave goodbye, but she had already gone back inside.

The plane ride to Korea jostled us in our seats. Pale bolts of lightning lashed the sky. Cardamom spent the journey exclaiming to herself as she looked out the window, while Sage studied the safety pamphlets. Uncle read from a book called *The Catching and Collection of Butterflies, Volume 3*, while taking notes in a small, leather-bound notepad.

A shiny black car pulled up to the airport when we landed. After what felt like hours of driving—on highways that cut past jagged skylines, then on bumpier routes through villages, then on packed dirt roads winding around fields—the car slowed to a stop before a mansion of steel and glass. The chauffeur whispered to an intercom on a tall gate. After a moment, the iron slid open, and the car passed through. We turned around to watch the gate slide back into place, sealing us away from the outside world.

On our first day in the house, Uncle told us we would be required to join him for breakfast, lunch, and dinner, but that otherwise we would be left to our own devices. He would be spending most of his time in the library. He showed it to us, and in spite of ourselves, we were enchanted. It was clear that Uncle's library was the beating heart of his home, its secret center. The library air was always dry, and the furnishings were comfortable and inviting. Bookshelves lined the walls from floor to ceiling. Over-stuffed couches and armchairs beckoned to us, and a plush car-pet the color of moss muffled our footsteps.

Uncle told us that his wife, a great reader, had helped him design the library. They had only been married for a few years when she died in childbirth. We asked, "What happened to the baby?" and he told us, "She died too. She would have been six-teen this year." A faint line appeared between his brows at the remembrance of his family, before it disappeared and he looked, once more, like an old tree.

Unlike the other rooms of the house, the large library win-dows had curtains, which were always drawn to protect Uncle's collection of butterflies. He kept the butterflies mounted and labeled in cases with gold clasps and fixtures, shining like jewels behind the glass, their wings and antennae spread as though in midflight.

Uncle had met his wife in a butterfly exhibit when a red admi-ral landed on her shoulder. He stopped to admire it, and then he stopped to admire her. When she smiled, he told us—his voice suddenly and unusually rough with feeling—it was even more beautiful than when a butterfly opens its wings for the first time. After they got married, he bought specimens from col-lectors around the world and mounted them himself in secret, carefully inserting a pin through each butterfly's stomach and using thin strips of paper to hold them down while they dried, and on their first anniversary he presented his wife with the col-lection, hoping she would be pleased. But she had begun to cry, disturbed by their unnatural, lifeless beauty. The two of them did not speak of the butterflies again, but Uncle, still obsessed with their symmetry and jeweled colors, continued to add to

the collection, despite his wife's consternation. With every mis-
understanding or difference that revealed itself between them,
he became more fixated on the butterflies, the preservation and
mounting of them, the way that each meticulous step resulted in
something that would live forever.

He showed us a new specimen he had just received, a spice-
bush swallowtail. Its ribbed black wings gleamed like oil underneath the amber light of Uncle's desk lamp as he slid the pin
through. Its wings seemed to tremble with pain, and despite ourselves, we reached our hands out to touch the butterfly's wings,
to comfort it, and Uncle slapped our hands away so hard that,
for a few seconds, we couldn't feel the red-hot sting that followed
the blow.

"You must never, never touch," he spat as we shrank back.

"We saw it move!"

He said, "That's impossible. It's already dead," but that was not
true, because all the butterflies were awake now. We felt their
eyes on us, heard the rustling of their wings against the pins that
kept them fastened to the foam backing of their cases. Uncle
seemed unaware of the thousands of small movements that rippled throughout the library as each of the butterflies—from the
giant Queen Alexandra's birdwing to the western pygmy blue, no
larger than one of our thumbnails—stirred and fluttered.

"I will tell you this once, and I will not tell you again," Uncle
said later, at dinner. Cardamom and Sage had been left upstairs,
because Uncle said we were not to have our dolls with us at the
table. Droplets of seaweed soup clung to his mustache. "Grime
and noise and misbehaving of any kind are unacceptable in this
house. Little girls should be quiet and obedient."

"You're not the boss of us," we said. "We want to go home."

As though we had not spoken, Uncle said, "You will wear the

clothes I pick for you. You will eat when I tell you to eat, and you will go to bed when I tell you to sleep. Anytime you disobey me or speak out of turn, you will be sent to your room without dinner. In fact, you can go upstairs now."

We pushed our bowls away and left the table, but our stomachs growled in our beds that night, and one of us wondered if perhaps we should have thought this through, even though the other shushed her.

On our second day in the house, when we went downstairs for breakfast, we were greeted with empty plates. Uncle ate a pile of fried eggs and toast. "If you would like to join me for breakfast, you can begin by apologizing for your rudeness," he said, between bites. We sat in silence, watching the eggs disappear from Uncle's dish, one by one. They shone like eyes.

It was the same at lunch, and again at dinner. That night, our stomachs shrank, twisting themselves into painful knots. We dreamt that the knots burst into vines, which grew up and out of our throats, choking us. We dreamt of a long table laden with food, at which our mother presided. "Mother!" we called. When she looked up, there was a smooth blankness where her mouth should have been.

We woke in the middle of the night drenched with sweat, and decided it was time to compromise. We drew ourselves our first bath in weeks. The water turned brown from the layers of dirt that had accumulated on our skin, and we combed shampoo through our hair, detangling it. Soap got in our eyes and made them sting. When we emerged from the bath, we felt smaller.

We put on the matching nightgowns we found in the chest of drawers in our room and stared at ourselves in the bathroom mirror. Cardamon said, "Lo and behold. The caterpillars have changed." Sage told us, "A caterpillar spends its whole life yearning to become. It builds itself a house of its longings, a shroud to its childhood, and when it is ready, it appears new, dressed in the finest gown money can buy. And then, after a year of honey and sun, it perishes, its wings beating slowly until they are stilled forever."

We considered Uncle's butterflies. They were allowed to live on in a kind of frozen eternity of beauty and color, yet what were they but exhibits in a museum of death? "What happens to the caterpillars who don't want to change?" we asked.

"They must stay close to the ground," Sage said, after thinking a while. "And creep slowly through the undergrowth, staying quiet and hidden. And that is how they will survive."

The next morning, we sat down to breakfast, wearing the neatly pressed dresses that had been hanging in our closet. Uncle looked up from his customary plate of eggs.

"We're sorry," we said. "May we eat now?"

He studied us before nodding and returning to his book. Mrs. Lee, Uncle's housekeeper, set two bowls of porridge down in front of us. We were so hungry we were tempted to lick our bowls clean, the way we would have back at home, but we restrained ourselves. When we were done, we said, "Is there more?" and Uncle told us, "That's enough for now."

Our stomachs sank into the bottoms of our shoes.

Our days in the glass house were slow but relentless. From the beginning, the place did not want us there. The cold walls sighed away from our touch, and the floors grew knots that tripped us when we went running down the corridors. The narrow modern side tables and low-slung chairs sharpened their angles when we walked past, so that our knees and elbows snagged on their corners. The doors either stuck in their frames or refused to stay shut, peeling themselves open unexpectedly, and the hallways echoed with the sound of footfalls that were never there when we turned around. Some days, we would throw our clothes out the windows, leap off chairs into piles of cushions, or howl down the halls, just to see if the house would take notice. But it seemed only to absorb our noise into itself. Despite all its glass, the house was shrouded in a permanent semidarkness, having been built on the side of a hill that faced away from the sun. In the dimly lit passageways, we saw indentations like faces that appeared and disappeared in the wallpaper. The dolls hated it. "This is the ugliest place we've ever seen," they said.

Uncle's library was the only part of the house that seemed to welcome us. We were not allowed there on our own, but we couldn't stop thinking about the butterflies, the spells they seemed to be under. And so, every day, during the still afternoon hour from three to four when Uncle napped, we stole into the hushed library darkness with the dolls, our whispers swallowed up by the shadows and dust, where the butterflies were waiting for us. Their wings trembled when we approached, like the eyelids of a restless sleeper. We tried to count them all and failed, usually losing count somewhere in the three hundreds.

Cardamom's favorite was the red lacewing. Its crimson-centered wings, with their black filigree borders, reminded us of a dress our mother had once worn to a party. It waved coquettishly at us, preening when we stopped to admire it. Sage's favorite was the Adonis blue. It was smaller than the red lacewing, not even half the size, and its wings glowed with a quiet, urgent blue that we had never seen anywhere else. We wanted to live inside that blue, to feel its coolness in our mouths and its powder on our fingertips.

We would stay in the library for as long as we dared, until we
heard the clock strike four. At night, we whispered the names of
the butterflies to each other over and over, savoring them. Purple
spotted swallowtail. Gold-drop helicopis. Danube clouded yellow. Long-tailed blue. Crowned hairstreak. Painted lady. Mourning cloak. They sounded like the ingredients in a magic spell.
Sometimes we imagined that if we whispered them to each other
fast enough, in the right combination, we would be free to go
home.

The housekeeper, Mrs. Lee, was a small, stoop-shouldered woman
with a round face and watchful, wide-set eyes. She arrived early
every morning but Sundays to cook and clean the glass-and-
steel house. She seemed afraid of Uncle, usually keeping her eyes
on the ground whenever he addressed her, but she often gave us
pitying smiles. During her breaks, she sat outside and smoked
cigarettes while speaking on the phone.

"I feel sorry for them," we heard her say one morning. "I don't
care how much money you have, it's just not a replacement for
family." The tinny voice on the other end of the line seemed to
ask a question, and Mrs. Lee snorted in response. "They may as
well be orphans. What kind of mother just dumps her kids for a
summer?"

Cardamom said, "I'd like to box her ears. What is an orphan,
anyway?" and Sage said, "An orphan is a type of fledgling bird
that has been left behind by its parents, often found in deciduous
forests or swamplands."

We told the dolls sternly, "We are not orphans." We decided
to leave an enormous dead beetle we had found in the garden in
Mrs. Lee's purse. After that, she no longer smiled at us, and she
made sure not to have her lunchtime phone conversations in our

earshot. After we tried to steal food from the kitchen to store in our room, she locked the pantry door.

So—we complied. We got used to things. We became accustomed to the confining clothes Uncle bought for us, the tightness of their zippers and buttons and fastenings, which kept us from moving about freely. Our stomachs shrank to the size of seeds. One of us tried learning to lower her voice. The other practiced walking in small, careful steps everywhere she went, instead of shouting and careening down the hallways like normal. We bathed every day, until we only smelled like flowers, or soap. When we walked past mirrors or saw our reflections in the windows of the glass house, we were smaller, prettier, less.

We wrote to Mother every day, enclosing drawings of the house and everything inside it. We drew pictures of the butterflies; the large, glacier-green celadon vases that stood throughout the house like soldiers; the sea-urchin chandeliers that clawed their way out of the ceilings. "We hate Uncle," we wrote. "He is mean to us and restricts our food. Please come at once." Mother never responded.

Monsoon season began. It rained almost every day, the sky an open wound that would not heal. The grasses and flowers in the backyard grew lush and feral. The trees turned an electric green. Fat worms wriggled up from the earth and found their way onto the stone in the courtyard in front of the house, where they dried up and turned into membranes when the sun came back out. The butterflies in the library grew more restless than ever, struggling against their pins, a constant tremor in their wings. Everything wanted to live.

We began to change. Our breasts felt tender and tingly, the way we imagined new buds in spring might. We wondered if the rain had something to do with these changes, if the inescapable fecundity of the earth and trees and flowers had somehow seeped into our bodies.

But when we stood before each other, we noticed discrepancies that disturbed us. One of us developed contours and curves in places where there had only been lines and corners before, while the other grew tall and angled. The blush-colored birthmark that only one of us had flushed into a dark strawberry, while the face of the other one broke out in angry red stars.

Even our reactions to the new differences were different. The possibility that perhaps we were not a single, split self frightened one of us, and gave the other a small thrill.

We no longer dreamt in unison, and when we woke in the mornings, we found ourselves facing away from each other, our bodies growing in separate directions. And every day, the dress of one of us grew tighter and tighter, while the other's grew shorter. It felt like just breathing would split our clothes open from seam to seam.

One morning, one of us woke to find a sticky, brownish patch of blood between her legs and strange aches in her stomach.

"She's dying!" Cardamom wailed, wringing her cloth hands.

"It's called a period," Sage said calmly. "It means that the balloon of blood that is your body has expelled the sorrows of the previous month, and now it is time to collect more."

We ran for Mrs. Lee. She clucked over us, a temporary truce declared over the pillowy pads she pulled from her purse. She didn't say how to use them, just told one of us, "You're a woman now," and left us alone to this terrible news. We puzzled over the white wings and determined that the gluey side must go on our skin. Both of us tried them on and winced when the stickiness ripped away the few hairs we had managed to grow down there.

The one of us who didn't need the pad said, "This feels like a diaper. You look like a big baby."

The other one said, "You're just jealous," and it was like a slap we had both been waiting for.

We wrestled, hitting and biting and kicking each other in a way we hadn't since we were too young to know any better. Bruises bloomed around our eyes, and our noses gushed red. Our forearms bore jagged scratches from each other's nails.

We stopped when one of us began to cry, stricken by the unaccustomed silence of the dolls. Sage's face was as mute and opaque as tinted glass, and Cardamom's arms were still, frozen in an attitude of panic, the anguished expression on her face replaced by a blankness we had never seen before. We shook them, slapped them, begged them to answer us, but they were as silent as graves. We were, truly, all alone.

At breakfast, we shifted in our chairs. *Are you okay?* we tried to ask each other, but there was a difference separating our minds—a barrier as thin and translucent as paper, but a barrier nonetheless.

During Uncle's afternoon nap, we snuck into the library to see the butterflies. They seemed to know, fluttering their wings in distress as we wept in front of their cases.

The Queen Alexandra's birdwing rattled behind its glass. *Free us,* it seemed to say. *Free us, and yourselves. We can make it stop, and you will stay the same forever.* We looked at each other, immensely relieved, each seeing that the other had heard the words as well. Outside, the monsoon roared; sheets of water washed over the house.

"Where will you go if we free you?" we asked. "You are not even alive."

We are also not dead.

"Uncle will punish us."

Are you not already being punished? The birdwing pulsated with thwarted life.

We hesitated only a few more seconds before one of us—we don't remember which one—picked up a marble paperweight and leveled it against the glass of the birdwing's case. A thin crack appeared, spiderwebbing across the surface. The other butterflies whispered amongst themselves, their chatter growing ever more excited as the glass continued to crack, before shattering. The birdwing struggled against its pin. We hastened to remove it, our thumbs pinched against the foamed plastic. Once the birdwing was free, it burst into the air like a coiled streamer.

It stretched its wings tentatively, seeming frightened by its sudden mobility. Then it flew around the library, arching its pierced thorax toward the vaulted ceiling. It rippled, aquamarine and black, a victory banner. It said, *Free. Be free.*

We smashed the rest of the butterfly cases, removing the pins as fast as we could. Glass shards crunched underneath our feet and cut both our hands and arms. Red seeped and dripped from our fingers as we unpinned each of the butterflies in Uncle's collection. Our fingers blistered, and we sucked the blood from them as we moved in unison from one case to the next. The sound of wings filled the air, a syncopated symphony of light and color. Soon the library was a fury of wings. Hundreds and hundreds of Uncle's butterflies soared to meet one another in midair.

"What are you doing?" Uncle shouted from somewhere far away. We caught a glimpse of him, a small irate figure standing in the doorway of the library, before the butterflies descended. The last thing we heard was Uncle's screams as the butterflies covered him with their jeweled bodies.

The Queen Alexandra's birdwing landed on one of our shoulders, and we felt a shudder run through us. Our thoughts ran together easily once more, braided like twin bolts of lightning. Pain jackknifed down our shoulder blades and spines as our bones cracked, turning to powder—red, yellow, blue, green. Our limbs telescoped, our faces beveled, our eyes grew large and kaleidoscopic.

Outside, it had stopped raining. The earth steamed with heat. We stretched our new wings, studying each other and ourselves, two halves of the same butterfly, a familiar, diamond-shaped spot the only thing that disrupted our symmetry. The air sparkled, zippy with ozone. We dripped with newness.

Are you ready? said the birdwing.

We left, together, flying out into a world of color and light, honey and sun.

You'll Never Know How Much I Loved You

Jiyeon was born a large child, ruddy of face and capacious of lung. "This one thinks she's a singer," the doctor said, noting how long and heartily Jiyeon wailed, as though she was determined to sustain the one note she knew. When her mother told her to hush, she did, and her parents rejoiced that they had been blessed with such an obedient daughter, although her mother noted, with some displeasure, that she was rather plain-looking.

By the time Jiyeon was three, she was singing songs from the radio, including pop ballads and old folk songs that made her grandmother cry, songs about lovers abandoning their women on mountainsides and hometowns left behind forever. She sang in a full, vibrating voice that sounded more suited to a grown woman than to a little girl.

Her parents were perturbed by this. "How can a child carry so much feeling in her voice?" they said.

"Children know more than we think they do," her grandmother retorted. "It's clear that this child has lived five lifetimes already."

It was true that Jiyeon was a bit old-womanish in her tastes and habits. As a child, she worried often, rotating her three favorite dolls frequently during playtime so that no one would feel left out. She even walked like her grandmother, who had a bad left foot—a slow shuffle. She did not play with the other children on their street, preferring to stay indoors and listen to the radio.

Jiyeon was five when her younger brother, Jimin, was born. He was as undersized as she had been large—a premature baby, but more important, a son. Jiyeon peered into the bundle that her mother brought home and felt shocked that anything could be so small. Her brother had tiny fists and a tongue like a kitten's. When she saw her mother nursing him, she was gripped by a longing to be nursed as well, to be held in the basket of her mother's arms.

"Don't be stupid," her grandmother said when she confided this to her. "Being a baby is terrible. That's why they cry all the time."

Jiyeon's grandmother had a face like a dried leaf and two bright eyes like coins, and Jiyeon loved her most of all. At bedtime, she would tell Jiyeon and Jimin stories about wandering tigers, crane wives, daughters of blind men who sacrificed themselves to the roar of the ocean out of filial piety. When Jiyeon had trouble sleeping, which was often, her grandmother would lie down beside her and sing to her in her low, husky voice, tracing patterns and letters across her back with her gnarled old fingers. Jimin, on the other hand, could never stay awake long enough to hear the ends of their grandmother's stories, and Jiyeon preferred it that way. She didn't mind having a younger brother who monopolized her parents' attention, because she knew her grandmother's stories belonged to her alone.

Jiyeon's favorite stories were the ones her grandmother told her about her girlhood in northern Korea, before she and the rest of her family had been forced to flee for the south. She would pull out her prized lacquer box, which was inlaid with mother-of-pearl phoenixes, and open it to show Jiyeon the jewelry that she and her sisters had managed to sew into their hems and sleeves for the journey. There were heavy necklaces of onyx and jade, gold bracelets, pearl rings, coral earrings, and brooches in the shapes of flowers and animals. Jiyeon's favorite was an elephant studded with glittering white stones that had a tiny ruby for an eye, which her grandmother had worn on her wedding day.

One day, when she was twelve years old, Jiyeon came home from school sobbing after doing poorly on an oral exam. School did not come easily for her, the way it did for Jimin, who was already reading at an advanced level and did sums for fun at the breakfast table. "What are you crying for, child?" her grandmother said.

"I'll never amount to anything. I'll just be stupid forever, and I'll never win any prizes," Jiyeon wailed.

"Stop this at once," her grandmother scolded. She had little patience for tears.

But the next morning, she pinned the elephant brooch to the lapel of Jiyeon's school uniform. "It'll bring you wisdom and strength," she said.

"I can't wear your brooch, Halmuni," Jiyeon protested. "It's too precious."

Her grandmother gripped Jiyeon's shoulders tightly and stared at her with a fierceness that she usually reserved for growling dogs and the drunks who sometimes harassed her on her way to the market. "Listen to me. In this life, you must be your own prize, and then no one can take that away from you. You are far more precious than any stone or jewel. Now, don't let me catch you crying about such nonsense ever again."

Jiyeon nodded, suddenly almost afraid of the strength in her grandmother's hands. Later, when she was an adult, she would think about this moment often, as well as the fact that her grandmother had given birth to seven children, including Jiyeon's father, and buried four.

When Jiyeon was thirteen, her grandmother died quietly in her sleep, of an aneurysm. Her grandmother's room was turned into a playroom, and her things, including the lacquer box, were bundled away into the attic. Jiyeon sometimes imagined that she could still hear her grandmother's voice coming from the attic, cackling at her own jokes, and the slide and shuffle of her footsteps.

Most of the jewelry was set aside and kept safe in a locked chest in her parents' bedroom, but Jiyeon managed to sneak the elephant brooch out of the black silken pouch it was kept in and hide it underneath the neatly rolled bundles of her socks and underwear. At night, when she missed her grandmother so much that her loneliness felt like a weight sitting on her chest, crushing her ribs and squeezing her lungs, she would slip out of bed to retrieve the brooch and rub her fingertips across the smooth metal and stones until her eyes closed.

Jiyeon and her vocal talents went largely unnoticed outside of the family until she was fifteen, when she joined the school choir. The music teacher, Mr. Suh, was one of the younger teachers at school, and many of the girls giggled that he was handsome. He was tall and thin, and the collared shirts he wore, which were always too large for him, had a tendency to billow out at the back. When he stood in front of the choir to guide them through another rendition of the school song for their monthly assemblies, his shoulders jumped up by his ears, and his eloquent white hands fluttered through the air like birds.

"You have a beautiful voice, Jiyeon," Mr. Suh told her once after practice. "Has anyone ever told you that?"

Her heart dropped into her shoes. "No," she said, her hands growing cold, as they often did when she was nervous. Her parents treated her voice as though it was yet another anomaly, something about her that they accepted but did not quite understand.

"You have an immense talent," he said. "You must never forget that." For a moment, Jiyeon could hardly breathe. She flexed her stiff fingers against the pleats of her navy skirt and thanked him, before stumbling out of the room.

After that, singing in the choir, which she had always enjoyed, became her sole reason for being. She waited all day for practice, the back of her neck tingling as soon as they had all settled into their chairs and Mr. Suh walked in, his necktie askew and his hair rumpled. When she sang with the other students, her voice braiding with theirs in a swell of harmony that seemed to reach all the way up to the heavens, she felt a thrill she had never known, a sense of being able to exceed the limitations of her body to be part of something greater.

A few weeks into the semester, Mr. Suh asked her to stay behind after choir practice and presented her with a record. On the cover was a serene-faced woman with short hair and graceful shoulders, her sad eyes dusted with a shimmery shade of lavender that matched the ruffles of her dress. "Hye Un-i," read the letters on the front. "She's one of my favorites," he said. "She has a voice like yours—full of feeling."

Jiyeon tried to refuse, embarrassed by his generosity, but he insisted, saying that he had a friend who ran a record shop who gave him new albums for free. She nodded her thanks and bowed deeply before running out of the classroom and all the way back home. Her parents were still at work when she arrived, and Jimin was outside, playing with the neighborhood boys. She kicked her shoes off, not stopping to line them up neatly on the mat as she normally did, and raced into her father's study, where he kept the record player. The hiss and pop of the record frayed her nerves, until the sound of a forlorn harmonica, accompanied by a gentle guitar, filled the room.

"You'll never know how much I loved you / As the years go by / You will repent," sang Hye Un-i. Her plaintive voice throbbed like a violin on the high notes, lingering in the room long after the song was over.

Jiyeon listened to it over and over again. She played it with the volume cranked as high as she dared, and then turned it down until Hye Un-i's voice was just a whisper. From then on, it became a ritual for her to run home after school to listen to the record in secret. She enjoyed the privacy of it, the thrilling sadness that the song evoked in her—the way it made her feel like a girl in a movie, like someone who was nursing a secret love. In her boldest moments, she imagined that the song was a message from Mr. Suh to her, that he dreamt about her just as much as she dreamt about him. At night, she wrapped her blankets around herself tightly, pretending that they were his arms, and for the first time since her grandmother's death, she felt the veil of loneliness that seemed to surround her at all times dissipate, like mist on a hot day.

A few months later, when Mr. Suh was found to be having an affair with an older student named Eunhae and was dismissed, Jiyeon kept thinking about that moment after choir practice, and whether he had also given a record to Eunhae, who was beautiful but had a terrible voice. She would replay the scene in her mind and pretend that she had smiled graciously and thanked him, instead of running out of the classroom like a child. Then, she imagined, he would have offered to walk her home, and would have told her again how special she was. She glowed with shame and desire at the idea of it, at the memory of how fixed and insistent his gaze had been, his eyes fastened on hers.

Jiyeon's mother was an enterprising and practical woman. She knew that Jiyeon was unlikely to be popular with men. But she was not the kind of mother to punish her daughter for not being beautiful, as she was not beautiful herself. Instead, she sat Jiyeon down one day when the girl was twenty-two years old and told her what she could expect from life going forward.

"Your father and I are happy together because we are suited to each other. We are of similar family backgrounds and temperaments, and that is why we have been able to build up your father's family practice and make it run successfully," her mother said. Jiyeon's father was a family doctor, and her mother was his receptionist. They had met through a neighborhood matchmaker.

"It's important that you understand that romantic love is not something to expect or hope for," her mother continued. "One of your father's colleagues, Dr. Chang, has a son a few years older than you. Byungchul is planning to be a doctor as well."

Jiyeon nodded, unsure of where this thread of conversation was going until she realized that her mother was implying that she and Byungchul might marry someday. The heat of embarrassment flooded her cheeks.

"Byungchul and his parents are coming over this weekend for dinner," Jiyeon's mother said. "He's a nice boy, from a good family."

Jiyeon was not accustomed to being spoken to so directly by her mother, who usually treated her as though she were an afterthought to her brother. By then, her brother Jiimin was seventeen years old, and he was studying for his university entrance exams. He was planning to study engineering at Seoul National University. Neighbors and family friends spoke of Jimin admiringly, often asking their parents about him. They rarely asked after Jiyeon, who, not being a brilliant or particularly diligent student, had gone on to a middling women's university only a twenty-minute bus ride away from her parents' house, where she was studying English and Italian. She enjoyed the feeling of the foreign words in her mouth. English felt like a large, slippery silver fish that always seemed to wriggle out of her hands when she least expected it, and Italian felt airy and melodic, like a song heard from a far-off mountaintop. She practiced her English sometimes by singing along with the pop and rock records she found in the record stores of Itaewon, which were always located in seedy alleyways and side streets that her parents would have been horrified to see her in.

At dinner with Byungchul and his parents, Jiyeon kept her eyes on her plate and focused on not spilling soup down the front of her new dress, which her mother had laid out on her bed before their guests arrived. It was navy with white trim, exactly the sort of dress Jiyeon's mother preferred. It was a little tight around her shoulders, and the seams dug into her underarms. She could already feel the red marks they would leave.

Byungchul had a broad face and a receding chin, and his head was round, like a melon. He ate vast quantities of food in complete silence. "Byungchul works so hard. I try to get him to focus on something other than his studies, but he won't listen to me. It's a sickness. I worry endlessly," his mother said, sounding pleased and not at all worried.

Jiyeon tried to engage Byungchul in conversation after dinner, over tea and sliced fruit. "What kind of doctor are you going to be?" she asked.

"An anesthesiologist," he said, without hesitation. "They make the most money."

"Ah!" she said. She waited for him to ask her something about herself—what she was studying at university, what she liked to do for fun, what dreams she had for the future. But they sat in a thick silence, amid the chatter of their parents. She could feel her failure weighing on her, and she hurried to rescue them both by lobbing question after question at him. Did he like to read, or go for walks? Did he plan to stay in Seoul? Did he listen to music?

His answers were short, unremarkable. No, no, yes, and no, because he didn't have time to pursue hobbies like music. Hobbies. The word felt like a reproach to Jiyeon, who couldn't imagine life without records, the stolen hours when she would listen to the songs that lifted her out of herself, either in her father's study when her parents were out of the house, or in her room, with the record player she had saved up enough to buy for herself.

Finally, he asked her a question. "Would you like to stay in Seoul?"

She imagined it. A life spent in the city where she'd been born and raised, married to Byungchul or someone just like him, with two or three children, seeing her parents every weekend, over meals just like this one, while wearing ill-fitting, sensible dresses. A safe, comfortable life with few surprises and thrills, with no one to talk to about the music that bubbled up inside her like a secret spring. It sounded awful.

"I want to be a singer and see the world," she said. She had no idea where this had come from, and the moment she said it, she regretted it. She sounded silly, childish. But she enjoyed the momentary widening of Byungchul's eyes that her words had caused.

The next evening, Jiyeon's mother asked her at dinner what on earth she had meant by telling Byungchul she wanted to become a singer. Singing was not a suitable job, her mother said. Entertainment was for cheap, common women, the girlfriends and mistresses of gangsters and government officials, not good girls from good families.

Byungchul and his family did not visit again. Jiyeon's mother, undaunted, attempted to orchestrate meetings with other potential suitors, but Jiyeon rejected them all. Instead, she stayed holed up in her room, studying and listening to records, and surprised everyone, including herself, by finishing the term with top marks. Not that it mattered, as Jiyeon's mother told their relatives and neighbors, because Jiyeon would be married soon.

But as the years passed and nearly all of Jiyeon's cousins and school friends married and had children, Jiyeon remained single. There was always something wrong with the men her parents chose for her, or something about her that the men themselves did not take to. Her parents finally stopped badgering her once Jimin became engaged, to his college girlfriend, and at their wedding, she stood by in a lilac grown that did not suit her with the elephant brooch pinned to her chest.

"Where did you get that?" her mother asked later, her eyes drawn to the brooch. Jiyeon's fingers fluttered protectively around it, as though her mother would snatch it away from her. But before she could reply, her mother sighed and said, "I suppose you're old enough now to take proper care of it." Jiyeon felt both forlorn and defiant at this pronouncement, which she imagined was her mother's way of announcing that she had officially given up on Jiyeon's marital prospects.

It was this defiance that led her to, rather than sit around and mope at home, find a job as an office girl, where she answered phones, made tea and coffee, and occasionally translated English correspondence into Korean. While the married men on her floor made perfunctory passes at her, especially during the semi-annual company drinking parties, she grew adept at averting their wandering hands and soon earned a reputation for being competent, if dull. She knew several other office girls, including her friend Sumi, who slept with married men and managed to get gifts, pets, and even apartments out of their arrangements. "You can get married men to give you anything if you ask them at the right time," Sumi told her. But Jiyeon knew that the life of a kept girl, no matter how luxurious or thrilling it might seem, was not for her. In her heart of hearts, as foolish as she knew it was, she was still holding out for the kind of love that Hye Un-i sang about and that her mother had warned her not to expect—a love that would bring back the exhilaration she had felt with Mr. Suh, all those years ago.

On Friday nights, she and Sumi and the other girls went out to restaurants and bars to meet men, and usually, once everyone had had enough soju, someone would suggest heading out to a noraebang. She loved the flashing lights and sticky tables of the karaoke rooms, the tambourines and plastic-wrapped microphones, though she rarely volunteered to sing on her own. "Jiyeon's got a really great voice," Sumi told their group one night.

"That's not true," Jiyeon said, almost automatically.

"Stop with the false modesty," Sumi said, swatting her playfully. "I've heard you singing to yourself in the break room while making tea."

So, amid much teasing and cajoling, Jiyeon queued up an old song of Hye Un-i's and, standing up and shutting her eyes, sang her heart out. It was a sad ballad, the wrong kind of song for that evening. Afterward, the whole room erupted in drunken, surprised cheers. Her cheeks felt hot and her head throbbed.

"It's too bad you've got a face like that and a voice like that," said one of the men, after a moment of silence while they waited for the next song. "You could really be a star, you know."

"Thank you," Jiyeon said, so thrilled by the unaccustomed praise and attention that it didn't occur to her until much later, when she was back at home, to be offended.

When Jiyeon turned thirty, it was decided that she would spend a summer abroad, at her father's older sister's home in America, in a place called New Jersey.

"A change of scenery will do you some good," said her father.

"Perhaps, when she comes back, she'll be ready to come to her senses and settle down," said her mother, who disapproved of her working an office job among so many men, and with no ring to show for it.

"Bring back a handsome American husband for me, won't you?" Sumi said, hugging her at the airport.

Thus began the happiest summer of Jiyeon's life. Her aunt's house was capacious, with two floors and a basement. Everywhere Jiyeon looked, there were Americans, mostly white people with big hair and big teeth, who moved slow and talked fast. Her aunt was married to one of them, a broad-chested blond man who worked at a law firm in Manhattan and wore pastel ties and gold watches, and instead of children, they had two fluffy white dogs, Mimi and Kiki. Jiyeon's aunt had long, shapely nails and wore bathrobes around the house with nothing on underneath, as though she lived in a spa. "Now, don't go telling your parents I let you drink," her aunt often said, pouring her a glass of red wine at dinner.

Jiyeon learned how to take the bus into New York City on her own, which only took forty minutes without traffic. She soon got used to American currency, the way bus drivers never looked at you when you said hello or thank you, and how New Yorkers would push past you without a glance. She loved the press and noise of the crowds, the anonymity of being able to slip into any café, bookshop, or movie theater and feel like an entirely different person. Seoul was just as busy and bustling as New York, if not more so, but there she had always felt as though her parents and their family friends could be watching from behind a corner, waiting for her to make a fool out of herself. Here, she thought, she could be any young woman, free from the disappointments and expectations of her family, even if it was just for a few hours.

This was how she met Jack. On a suffocatingly humid July afternoon, she ducked into a dimly lit art gallery on the Lower East Side to avoid a sudden downpour. She was wearing a red dress that had been her aunt's, who had insisted that she start dressing more appropriately for her age. "You dress like a nun, Jiyeon," her aunt said impatiently. "This red will bring out the roses in your cheeks." She had tried to refuse, certain the dress wouldn't fit her, but it had. Jiyeon had felt an unfamiliar pleasure while regarding herself in the mirror that morning. The hem of the dress ended just above her knee, and the skirt flared out when she turned. The deep "V" of the collar revealed just a hint of cleavage, which she felt momentarily thrilled by, before she safety-pinned it closed. She impulsively pinned her grandmother's elephant brooch over her left breast, where it sparkled jauntily.

She adjusted the brooch now as she shook the raindrops off herself and tried to smile at the receptionist, who ignored her. The gallery was lined with small canvas squares, no larger than the palm of her hand, filled with marbled layers of color. They looked like the ridged waves of an ocean, but in shades like acid green, scarlet, and bright purple. She stood rooted to the middle of the room in wonder, surveying the colors around her.

"Can I help you?" a man in a sharp gray suit with pomaded black hair asked her. He appeared to have materialized from nowhere. He had broad cheekbones, narrow eyes, and a finely chiseled jawline, and though his face was unlined, threads of gray streaked his temples. When he saw her face, he switched into Chinese, and she shook her head, smiling. He spoke to her again in Korean, and after a moment of surprise, she replied in kind, saying that she was just waiting until the rain stopped so she could catch the bus back home.

"And where's home?" he asked her. His cheekbones seemed to come into even sharper relief when he smiled. She noticed that he was not wearing a wedding ring, and that his black shoes, though well polished, were scuffed. "I'm staying at my aunt's in New Jersey for the summer," she said.

"New Jersey. A fine place," he said, with a hint of irony. "I'm just about to close up for the day. Would you like to get a drink with me?"

His name was Park Jaebeom, but his friends called him Jack. He told her that he didn't own the gallery, but a family friend did. "I basically run the place," he said, in a tone that she could tell was meant to sound offhand. "I'm saving up to buy it from him once he retires." He was also a painter, he told her. He worked in a rickety studio in Brooklyn. Sometimes he even slept there, because, as he said, you never knew when the muse would strike.

They sat on bar stools next to each other, so close their knees were almost touching. She asked him where he had learned Chinese. He traced a white circle on the wooden table with one finger while he told her that, though his parents were from Korea, he'd been born in Beijing, and when he was six, he had moved to New York City with his parents, who ran a laundromat in Chinatown.

She drank her bitter-tasting beer, the bubbles rising inside her throat like tiny balloons, and thought dizzily to herself that here she was, Kim Jiyeon, sitting in a bar talking to a handsome older man who had seen so much more of the world than she had. She told him that she had liked the paintings in the gallery. "They reminded me a little of Rothko. Do you paint things like that?" she asked.

Not a muscle in his face moved, but something about his easy smile turned cold, like a momentary chill on a warm summer day. "Rothko would spit on those paintings if he saw them," he said. "They're completely unoriginal." She felt the weight of her mistake, and her aunt's red dress suddenly felt too tight on her.

"Once I take over, we won't be showing second-rate work of that kind anymore. But you've finished your drink," he said, the quick zip of his scorn suddenly gone from his voice. "Let me get you another." He complimented her brooch, remarking on how unusual it was. Over her second glass, she found herself telling him about her life—her grandmother, her parents, their failed attempts at getting her married off, her brother's brilliance, her love of music. He listened with a quiet intensity that she had not felt directed at her since Mr. Suh, and she realized that, even if she was starting to get drunk, the heat suffusing her body and rushing to her skin could not be blamed on the beer alone.

The bar smelled like oranges. Outside, the rain had stopped and the streetlights had blinked on, their amber light buttery and soft through the speckled glass windows of the bar. Jiyeon realized with a start that she had missed her usual bus back home.

She began to make her excuses, and Jack hailed a cab for her. It splashed gray water onto the curb as it pulled up, just missing the hem of her skirt. "Thank you for the drink," she said, and because she didn't know what else to do, she stuck out her hand. He took it, grasping her fingers firmly.

"If you were an American girl," he said, "I'd ask when I could see you again."

"It's too bad I'm not, then," she said, and blushed at her own boldness. He grinned back at her, before turning her hand over to kiss the back of it. The brush of his lips on her skin sent a shiver through her body.

"Come see me again," he said.

At Port Authority, when she dug into her purse to find her bus ticket, her fingers closed around a small square of soft paper that had been tucked into the back pocket, somewhere between her wallet and the pocket mirror she kept in her purse even though she never remembered to consult it. It was a napkin, stamped with the name of the bar. Rendered in hasty blue ink across its folds and wrinkles was a drawing of her, or of a woman whose short, bobbed hair and open-collared dress seemed to belong to her. He must have tucked the napkin into her purse when she wasn't looking. The woman's face had been left obscured, lightly shaded in, but the curve of her neck and the placement of her hand against her cheek seemed to indicate that she was gazing directly at the viewer. She looked elegant, stylish, and at ease, in a way that Jiyeon could only hope to emulate.

A crying child and his scolding mother boarded the bus, as did a group of giggling teenagers whose laughter only intensified when the bus driver told them to be quiet. The sounds of late-night traffic, a cacophony of horns and sirens, punctuated the noise of the other passengers. But Jiyeon heard none of it, and the glittering lights of the city receded behind her as she examined every inch of the crumpled napkin, and imagined Jack's fingers remembering her.

Jack had never finished college, a fact he seemed to be both proud and ashamed of, but he enjoyed being more knowledgeable than Jiyeon in matters of the world, and she allowed him to play teacher. He wooed her over sunset walks across the Brooklyn Bridge, dinners in the West Village, and weekend picnics in Central Park, where he showed her the secret rivulets and glades he liked to sketch or paint in sometimes. White and yellow plastic bags rustled underneath their shoes when they walked off the bike paths, and the ponds were often frosted with algae as thick and green as old cake frosting. But she found almost everything unbearably beautiful when she was with him.

Jack's parents still lived in the same Chinatown tenement they had been lucky enough to rent for cheap back when they first moved to the States. He spoke proudly of the sacrifices they had made for him and his brother, but she gathered that he was a little ashamed of them, in the way of men who were determined to seem successful and self-made.

Jiyeon's aunt, sensing that something had changed, sniffed out that a man had entered the picture, and Jack was invited to the house in New Jersey for dinner. The evening was a great success. Jiyeon's aunt loved him, squealing over how handsome he was and openly flirting with him at dinner in a way that made Jiyeon uncomfortable but that seemed to please everyone else. Even her parents, when she spoke with them on the phone about having met someone, were pleased. "I always knew sending her to America was the best thing," her mother said.

They were slightly apprehensive when she told them that Jack was an artist, although their fears were somewhat alleviated when she told them that he managed an art gallery for a family friend. "He's very good at his job. He's an excellent salesperson," she said. She had practiced how she would explain Jack's profession, which was a far cry from the orderly lineage of doctors and scholars in her own family. This seemed to satisfy her parents, who gave their blessing when Jack proposed to her at the end of the summer, a week before she was to return to Korea. He did so without ceremony or visible nervousness, and when she said yes, he kissed her on the forehead. It bothered her a little, this kiss, though she could not articulate why.

They were married twice, first in Seoul in October and then in New York City in November. Jiyeon's parents paid for everything, and Jack's parents only attended their New York City wedding. They seemed much smaller than their son, his father in a shiny, ill-fitting rented suit and his mother in an old hanbok that she must have brought with her from Korea years ago. They seemed overwhelmed by the multicourse dinner and the complicated floral arrangements, all of which Jiyeon's mother had seen to. Jack's mother seemed a decade older than Jiyeon's mother, even though they were around the same age. She grasped Jiyeon's hands in hers. "Thank goodness he's found you," she said.

"Just remember that you have to be careful with a good-looking man" was the only thing Jiyeon's mother said to her, the morning of the wedding. "They have a hard time saying no to other people."

Jiyeon quelled the pulse of annoyance she felt at this and thanked her mother as she adjusted her elaborate hairdo in the mirror. She missed her grandmother. She felt sure that her grandmother would have enjoyed Jack, his good looks and his quick ways. She fingered the elephant brooch, which she kept in her clutch that day for good luck, running her fingertips over the stones as though she were praying. "Halmuni, I've found the most wonderful man, and he loves me," she imagined saying to her grandmother. But, despite her best attempts to conjure up her grandmother's voice in reply, all she heard was the nervous patter of her own heart.

Jack's art-world friends—turtlenecked Americans with long faces and outlandish eyewear—did not come to the wedding, but sent odd gifts, like novelty toasters and undulating ceramic vases. Jiyeon dutifully displayed them in their cramped Upper West Side apartment alongside her treasured record player and albums. Jack tried to turn her on to cassettes, bringing home boxes of tapes from artists like the Cranberries, Madonna, Bryan Adams, and the Pretenders. She liked his music, and even liked the little yellow Walkman he got for her, but she preferred the gentle hiss of her records, the way the music felt like a magic trick whenever the needle caught. "My little old lady," Jack said fondly.

Jack taught her how to enjoy alcohol, and how to take tiny sips of it to taste all the notes he insisted were part of the dark wines and beers he brought home, many of them left over from art openings at the gallery. He also taught her how to dance, in their tiny living room. She worried that the neighbors below them would hear, especially because they had to move their coffee table and the lone armchair to dance, but she loved the press of his hand against the small of her back and the sound of his off-key humming in her ear as he steered her gently around their threadbare carpet.

Sometimes they held parties in the little apartment, for Jack's friends. These were raucous gatherings, filled with cigarette smoke and too many glasses of rum punch. Jack's friends rarely spoke to her for longer than a minute at a time, perhaps because she could never project her voice loud enough to be heard over the music. By then, she was working part-time as a receptionist at her uncle's law firm in midtown, and one December she decided to invite one of the other receptionists, a red-haired woman named Gwen. She was not particularly attached to Gwen, who was forever complaining about either her ex-husband or her young son, and Jiyeon had invited her primarily out of a desire to prove to herself that she had a life outside of their marriage.

Gwen showed up to the party dressed in a tight reindeer sweater, already quite tipsy, her hair freshly dyed a brassy blond color that gleamed in the dim lamplight. Jiyeon thought nothing of it when Gwen flirted with Jack, who, like most handsome men, took her attentions in stride. She was used to the way women, especially white women, treated her husband. It was different from how they would treat a white man, because with Jack, it was assumed, there was no danger of his actually daring to take them seriously. So when Gwen placed her hand on his shoulder to emphasize a point she was making, or when Jack's hand hovered over the small of Gwen's back on his way to the kitchen for fresh liquor, Jiyeon dismissed the nagging sensation at the bottom of her stomach that said she should feel bothered by this.

She had told Jack, a month or so into their relationship, about her youthful ambitions to become a singer, and about Mr. Suh's comments to her, which she continued to hold close to her heart, like a candle in danger of blowing out. Jack asked her to sing for him, and she declined. "I don't want to disturb our neighbors," she said. She still hummed along to records and tapes at home, but there was nothing she could do in their apartment, with its thin walls, that their neighbors wouldn't hear, and singing felt like a social violation. After all, it was not like an instrument that you could pick up or put down as you pleased, like the guitar or the violin, both of which various neighbors in their building practiced. These musical interludes from other residents never felt like interruptions or pleas for attention, in the way that she felt singing did.

But the truth was that she was afraid of singing in front of Jack. He had been amused by the information that she could sing, the way he often was in those days at learning anything new about her. He often commented on small behaviors or quirks she had not known she possessed, such as her dislike of blue plates, or her terrible sense of direction. His quick eyes seemed to take in the measure and sweep of her limbs whenever she moved across the small yet well-traveled stage of their life, a circular route from home to work to the art gallery, where she sometimes visited Jack during the day. She sometimes felt that he was appraising her, the way he would study a new work or arrangement in the gallery, tilting his head to determine whether something belonged, and she feared that her singing voice would not fit in with his conception of her, just as almost everyone, including her parents, found her singing incongruous, even disturbing.

And then, one day, a day she could not affix in her memory as belonging to any particular month or time of year but which she felt as acutely as she did the changing of summer to fall—a new chill in the air, a hushed quality to the way twilight descended— Jack's eyes stopped following her as keenly as they once had. She chalked this up to his busyness—the gallery had had a run of successful shows, and Jack was forever having to attend events around the city "to see and be seen," which he told her she didn't have to come to with him. Perhaps this was simply what happened in a marriage—the slow slide into an intimacy that also meant familiarity and sameness.

She called her mother from time to time, and whenever her mother inquired about Jack, she gave her the same answer. "He's doing very well," she said, which seemed true enough. She did not mention that they barely saw each other unless she roused herself to go to an event at the art gallery; that often he was just falling into bed, smelling of whiskey and wine and cigarettes, when she was about to wake up. "He works so hard," she told her parents.

One morning, she woke up and knew with absolute certainty, when she rolled over on her side to face Jack, that he was lying to her. She couldn't divine precisely what it was he was deceiving her about, but she felt it in every fiber of her body, as clearly as she could smell his morning breath as he slept, unaware of her scrutiny.

Was he seeing another woman? Had a business dealing gone awry? Had he been gambling? She ran through the inventory of every possible husbandly crime in her mind before deciding that none of them were exactly right. She was surprised by her own ability to be dispassionate about this, as though he were no longer her husband but a hypothetical person in a hypothetical situation that did not involve her at all.

When he woke, he smiled to find her gazing at him so intensely. "Morning," he said. A lurch went through her stomach, and she saw green. She barely made it to the bathroom and retched water and bile into the toilet while Jack called after her.

When she came back to bed, she felt bone-weary. He wrapped his arms around her and nestled his chin into the space between her neck and head. "It's nice to have your wife immediately start vomiting when you say good morning to her," he said.

She laughed weakly. "I think I'm pregnant," she said.

During her pregnancy, she became keenly aware how very few people there were who looked like her in their neighborhood. She craved the foods of her childhood, but to buy ingredients like pepper paste, daikon radishes, or sticky rice, she had to take the train all the way out to Queens. She enjoyed looking into the wrinkled faces of the old fruit vendors on the street who tried to speak to her in Mandarin, and who reminded her of the neighborhood elders of her own childhood. They gave her extra produce when they saw the gentle swell of her belly beneath her housedresses. "For the baby," they said to her in English, when she tried to pay them.

Jack greeted the news of her pregnancy with characteristic equanimity, though she could tell he was ecstatic when they found out it would be a boy. He had given up the studio in Brooklyn, as the gallery required more and more of his attention following his promotion to director. With a loan from Jiyeon's parents, they were able to move to a house in the suburbs, in a town not far from Jiyeon's aunt and uncle.

Arthur was a fussy baby, given to wailing for extended periods of time, which had led to complaints from their elderly neighbors in Manhattan. But in New Jersey, a disturbing new development took hold, far more unsettling than the tenacity and strength of Arthur's cries. Periods of darkness began to descend on Jiyeon. She was often alone in the house with the baby, while Jack worked in the city. She would stand in their living room, nursing Arthur, and wonder what would happen if she left him in the bathtub and walked out their front door and into the street. She had dreams in which she abandoned Arthur on park benches or at bus stations, and when she woke from them, she was always soaked with sweat and tears. She would run to the crib and choke back her sobs of relief to see Arthur asleep right where she had left him.

She did not confide any of this to Jack, who slept soundly throughout their first few months with Arthur. She did not begrudge him his sleep, telling herself that he needed to rest. There was always a new exhibit to attend to, another biennial or retrospective that he needed to show his face at. She no longer tried to accompany him on these trips, or even on evenings out in the city. Breast-feeding deflated her, leaching the pounds off her waist until she was finally at the weight that her mother had always wanted for her, though she felt as though her skin now hung on her in folds, her body a vague and uncertain shape.

The only thing that seemed to soothe Arthur during his fits of outrage at the world were her old Hye Un-i records. Hye Un-i's lilting, tremulous soprano eased her mind as well, and reminded her of the young girl she had once been, when her dreams and desires were far simpler, and less obscure to herself. She was reminded of that one happy summer when she had first met Jack, and when she had gotten a taste of what an independent life in a large city would look like.

She began crying at unexpected moments throughout the day, sometimes without realizing it—chopping vegetables, washing the dishes, folding the laundry. Arthur seemed to find her tears fascinating, often reaching one chubby hand up to touch her face, which only made her cry harder. Jack was uncomfortable with her tears. "What's wrong?" he'd demand, as though she'd told him her stomach hurt. She never knew how to answer him, because, she thought, it would be ungrateful and unreasonable of her to ask him to stay at home more often with her, or to introduce her to more people. It occurred to her for the first time in their five-year marriage that she was almost all alone in this country, near a city she had only just begun to understand, and, in contrast to how thrilled she had been by this fact years ago, it now frightened her, how solitary she truly was.

So, in a way, it was a relief when, one day, the doorbell rang while Arthur was asleep and she opened the door to another woman. "Can I help you?" she asked, with a tentative smile.

The woman was older, white, with dark-blond hair piled into a bun on the top of her head. She was wearing a coat, even though it was an unseasonably warm day in November. She looked Jiyeon up and down. "My goodness, you're young," she said.

"I'm sorry," Jiyeon said, trying to be polite. "We're not interested in buying anything."

"I think you and I had better talk," the woman said. "You see, I'm Jack's wife."

At first she was unable to understand what the woman, who said her name was Claire, was saying. She could only hear a ringing in her ears, and when the ringing finally stopped, she found that she was sitting on the couch, and Claire, who had taken off her coat, had gotten her a glass of water from her own kitchen, and the idea of this strange woman rummaging through her cupboards filled her with a white-hot rage. She noticed, with distaste, that the woman had not taken her shoes off to enter the house. She would need to mop the floors later.

"I was pretty shocked myself when I found out about you," the woman said.

"Found out about me?" Jiyeon said. She wondered if her English had failed her. Perhaps she had misheard.

Claire shook her head. "You better drink that water." Jiyeon detected a flatness in the woman's tones, an inflection that seemed quieter, yet broader than the New York and New Jersey accents she was used to and that she had started to hear echoes of in her own accent.

The story was simple enough. Jack and Claire had met in Chicago, where she still lived, years ago, not long after the death of Claire's first husband, a wealthy insurance salesman. Jiyeon felt a sickening sense of familiarity as Claire told her, briefly and simply, about what had transpired between them. How Jack had approached Claire first, at the art museum. "A Monet exhibit," Claire said, with a bitter smile. "I've always loved Monet."

He had asked her if she'd like to get a drink at a bar nearby. He told her that he was an artist, a painter who waited tables and lived from paycheck to paycheck while making art in New York City. He was in Chicago visiting friends. Soon after his trip was to end, he moved in with Claire. After a six-week courtship, they had gotten married at a courthouse. A few months later, he had asked her to loan him some money, because, he said, his mother was sick, and he couldn't afford the medication. Then his mother had died, and he'd asked Claire for more money, for the funeral.

"Should I come?" she'd asked.

"No, no," he said. "I'll be home soon."

But his calls and letters grew increasingly infrequent, until, finally, he stopped responding at all. Claire filed for divorce. However, she still wore the cheap ring he had given her, a bauble from a pawn shop that he had promised he would replace with a real diamond someday. She twisted it around and around on her finger as she told the story.

"What do you want?" Jiyeon said when she was done.

Claire looked at her with weary amusement. "Nothing at all, dear," she said. "I just thought you should know."

"You wouldn't have come all this way just to tell me that insane story," Jiyeon said. She gripped the glass of water in her hand, as though to steel herself from throwing it at this woman.

"I suppose I wanted to see him. Jack, I mean," Claire said. She folded her hands in her lap.

"You should leave," Jiyeon said.

"All I want," Claire said, sounding desperate for the first time, "is to see him. You have no idea how long it's taken for me to find him."

Upstairs, Arthur began to cry. Claire looked stricken. "Do you have children?"

Jiyeon sprang to her feet. "Please leave," she told the woman. "Or I will call the police."

Claire stood and gathered her things. Jiyeon noted dully that she was an attractive woman, far taller than Jiyeon, with a long, graceful neck. Her wrists smelled of a delicate perfume. Lilies, perhaps. "Tell him I came by, won't you?" she said, before Jiyeon closed the door and collapsed on the stairs. She listened dully to the sounds of Arthur's wails intensifying. Finally, she crept upstairs, where Arthur lay, red-faced from crying. She breathed in his milky scent and rocked him back to sleep.

Afterward, she mopped the floors and even scrubbed them on her hands and knees, until she felt confident that every last trace of the woman was gone. She wondered why Claire hadn't gone to Jack's gallery to see him first. Why bother coming all the way out here, if she was so determined to talk to him? Then she realized that the woman hadn't been able to help herself. She had wanted to see her, Jiyeon, and the traces of the life that she herself might have known.

Later, when Jack came home from work, Jiyeon found, to her shock, that someone else seemed to have taken over her body. That someone else seemed perfectly capable of taking his coat and hat and hanging them up; tending to Arthur; setting out soup, rice, and side dishes for dinner; and making nonsensical small talk about the events of the day, while the real Jiyeon lay somewhere facedown in a puddle at the bottom of her stomach. "You're in a good mood tonight," Jack said over his second beer. She smiled and picked at her food. After dinner, they watched the evening news while she washed up and Jack played with Arthur. She turned the water as hot as she could stand it and scrubbed every dish until it squeaked beneath her fingers.

She fell asleep easily, like a stone sinking in deep water, but in the middle of the night, she bolted up in bed as though a ghost had called her name. Downstairs, she paced the kitchen floor, unable to reconcile her life—the house, her husband, her son— with what the woman from that afternoon had told her.

She picked up the phone a few times and listened to the dial tone. It was past midnight now. It would be afternoon in Korea. She imagined what her mother would be doing, if she would be setting out lunch for her father, or if they would perhaps go out to a restaurant together, as they were sometimes fond of doing. But what would she say if her mother picked up? That she, Jiyeon, had been a fool? That she was perhaps not even legally married to her husband? She hung up. She caught sight of her own reflection in the dark windows of their kitchen, her hair loose and her face sharp and pinched. She barely recognized herself.

The next morning, it had turned cold again. From the bedroom window, she could see that their tiny square of green lawn was now silvered with frost. She felt exhausted and wondered why, until she remembered.

She turned on her side to face Jack, who slept like a boy, his left arm flung out to one side and his right tucked underneath his pillow, as though he were trying to hold fast to something. How many times, on how many mornings, had she woken before Jack to regard him, just like this, marveling at her luck, her happiness? She studied his face, squinting as the gray morning light seeped into their tiny bedroom, wondering what exact arrangement of eye to nose to mouth to chin to jaw made a person desirable, made another person want to suffer for them, chase them halfway across the country even after being abandoned, just to see them again.

She recalled how, on a morning just like this, before Arthur was born, she had woken to the knowledge that Jack was lying to her. Would Claire's story have hurt her any more or less had she not felt that premonitory flash? She wished she had never invited her in. She should have shut the door in her face and brought it up to Jack, later, over dinner, as though it were something completely ordinary. "A woman came by today, looking for you." "For me?" "Yes, she kept saying she was your wife. I told her she must be mistaken."

She imagined sliding out of bed, throwing her clothes into a bag. Gathering the cash she kept in a jar in the kitchen, for emergencies. Strapping Arthur to her chest, calling a cab.

But then Jack woke up. His eyes fluttered open, and his breath warmed her face. "Good morning, my wife," he whispered, so as not to wake Arthur.

"I should go start breakfast," she said.

"Not yet," he said, drawing her close to him, and she bit her lip at how sweet it still felt, to be held in his arms. "Stay here with me."

The jar in the kitchen held about a hundred dollars. It would be enough for a train ticket to somewhere far away, if not a ticket to an entirely new life. Or she could ask her parents to wire her the money for a flight home. She could hang her head, tell her mother everything, and live bravely through the shame of having left her marriage. She could grab the few jewels she owned—her engagement and wedding rings, the freshwater pearls Jack had given her a few years ago, her grandmother's brooch—and sell them, use them to buy a way out. She could curse Jack's name, refuse to answer his calls (she wondered if he would indeed call, or bother to come looking for her), tell their son the truth when he was older, and turn him against his father.

She thought about what her grandmother had told her, all those years ago, her fierce gaze as bright as the elephant's ruby eye. *In this life, you must be your own prize, and then no one can take that away from you.* She could leave, and never again wonder what other lies there had been, and forget that she had ever been in love, that she had once believed herself to be loved in return. She could begin anew, trusting only in herself. And perhaps that would be enough.

"What are you thinking about, my little old lady?" Jack said tenderly.

But no. Her grandmother had been wrong. Jiyeon had never been anyone's prize, least of all her own.

She closed her eyes, so that he would not see her cry. "Nothing," she said. "I was just thinking about how much I loved you."

The Fruits of Sin

It was Mrs. Lee who first heard it from Mrs. Suh, who heard it in turn from Mrs. Park, who said she'd confirmed it with Mrs. Kim: that Reverend Chang's seventeen-year-old daughter, Sora—the skinny one who never looked anyone in the eyes and never did insa properly, barely bobbing her head downward in the most perfunctory way—was pregnant.

"Perhaps it's an immaculate conception, a second coming," the bolder among us said, tittering over hot Styrofoam cups of barley tea after services, taking care not to spill any on our patterned blouses.

"Who might the father be?" the rest of us wondered, telegraphing our curiosity to one another with our carefully plucked or tattooed eyebrows. We were none of us young anymore, and our eyesight was going, but very little escaped the attention of our eyebrows, which quirked upward at the first sign of gossip, like antennae.

Soon after we heard of Sora's condition, Reverend Chang, who often began Sunday services with prayer, stopped delivering the sermon. Instead, his assistant, Pastor Mark, who had recently graduated from seminary, commandeered the pulpit, while Reverend Chang sat on the side. We noticed that the reverend's thinning hair was, as always, combed neatly over his bald spot, but his lips pressed themselves into a white line of concern as Pastor Mark stumbled through the Bible verses in his terrible Korean.

Next to us, our husbands dozed, checked their phones, or impatiently flipped through the tissue-thin pages of our leather-bound Bibles for us when we couldn't find the daily scripture verses. We wondered when our husbands, these men we'd known for most of our adult lives, whose shirts we'd ironed and whose bellies we'd filled and whose children we'd borne without complaint, had become so old and crotchety and dull, and when they had started taking on that old-man smell, like sweaters left in a basement.

We studied Sora Chang, who sat in the front pew and didn't open her mouth once, not even to sing the hymns. Her hair, the only beautiful thing about her, hung long and straight down her back, its reddish-brown strands catching the light. When we were called to bow our heads to thank the Lord for another blessed week, we noticed that Sora didn't bother to close her eyes, instead keeping them cast up toward the ceiling, as though she were reading something fascinating there.

"She doesn't look very pregnant," we whispered to one another, and, indeed, Sora seemed to be as thin as ever, her bad posture turning her body into a lazy "C" hunched over itself.

We thanked God that our children were not like Sora. Before her disgrace, she was known for being a straight-A student at the local high school—bound for Harvard or Yale or at least

Princeton, we had all thought. She had been accepted into the regional and state youth orchestras every year, where she sat in the front row of the woodwinds section with her clear-tongued clarinet, her hair neatly combed into a French braid. Sora Chang had everything a girl in our community could want—a father with a respected position, brains, credentials, youth—only to throw it all away, and many of us considered this unforgivable.

We were grateful that our children were also not like Melody, the older Chang daughter, who had hair that, when she parted it, was completely shaved off on one side, like a prickly half-melon. Melody came to church only on holidays, wearing dark lipstick and dresses that didn't even make an attempt at hiding her tattoos. We heard that she no longer lived in the state, that she lived in a house in the country with—and this we only whispered over the phone to one another when our husbands, who disapproved of our gossiping, weren't listening—another woman. "Just like husband and wife," Mrs. Lee said, her surgically enhanced double eyelids almost disappearing as she widened her eyes at the scandal of it all.

Mrs. Lee also said that it was unconscionable for Reverend Chang to go on not addressing the fact that his unmarried daughter was continuing to come to church, week after week, with a belly that was gradually swelling with new life. "It's obscene," she said. "If Sora's mother was here, she would never have stood for this." Reverend Chang's wife had passed away when Sora was a little girl and Melody was a teenager, and the reverend had not remarried after her death.

"And what is the church for," said Mrs. Suh, "if we do not hold one another accountable, and root out the sinful among us?"

Others, like Mrs. Park, whose son Philip was back in rehab after stealing his father's car and running it into a median on the highway, ventured that didn't Jesus teach us that it was only he who was without sin who should dare to cast the first stone?

The rest of us went home that Sunday deep in thought. We thought about Mrs. Park's Philip, a good-looking boy who many of our daughters had been in love with, until he began drinking. Now he was puffy-faced and red-eyed, much heavier than he had been in his youth, but when he came back to church for Christmas or Easter, he always escorted his mother down the aisle to one of the best pews in the sanctuary, holding her gently by the elbow. Much of Mrs. Park's hair had fallen out after her radiation treatments, and her face, bloated with sickness, was waxy and yellow—we heard that she only had a few months left at most—but when she walked into the sanctuary with her son, she was radiant. *Here is my boy, who, despite his many mistakes, is still alive, and has never forgotten to love and honor his mother,* her proud smile seemed to say as they shuffled down the aisle together.

Many of the other churchgoers had shunned or pitied the Parks after Philip's accident, whispering amongst themselves that it was too bad that a nice boy had turned out so, and that perhaps it was due to Mrs. Park's having coddled him too much as a child. Mrs. Park herself never seemed ashamed of her son. At the end of each Sunday service, when Pastor Mark asked the congregation to submit their prayer requests, she would often pipe up to say, "I would appreciate it if you all would keep Philip in your prayers this week." And yet we knew that she often cried alone in her car in the church parking lot on Sunday mornings, before blowing her nose and dabbing at her eye makeup to emerge with a smile.

Other than Mrs. Park's Philip, most of our children were unremarkable in the ways they disappointed us. But whether it was

Mrs. Suh's Andrew getting caught palming dollar bills from his father's wallet, or Mrs. Kim's Esther leaving the church to become a Buddhist, or Mrs. Lee's Stephanie having to go to a community college after barely graduating from high school, we told one another that at least none of them had ever gotten pregnant or gotten anyone else pregnant.

We observed Reverend Chang closely and wondered what hidden pains he concealed underneath his ecclesiastical robes. He did not seem the type to cry openly, rend his clothes, beat his chest, or threaten his daughter with dire punishments, the way the fathers in our favorite Korean dramas did when their children shamed them. The only sign of consternation we could detect lay in the way he became increasingly sloppy when it came to brushing his hair over his bald spot, until, eventually, he forgot to attend to it at all, and his scalp gleamed like a doorknob underneath the lights of the church ceiling every week. We felt sorry for him, as we did for all wifeless men. Men without women, we thought, were like plants that had forgotten how to take in the sun. They grew droopy and bedraggled in times of crisis, completely unable to help themselves.

We considered, while we went through the routine of our weekdays—shopping, preparing meals, watching our dramas, ignoring our husbands' snores, calling our children to ask them when they'd be coming home next—how we would react if one of our own daughters were to sin in such an egregious way. Perhaps, we thought, it was better if the Changs were left alone to handle the matter directly, for didn't we know that all families operated according to their own language and logic? We all knew that Mrs. Suh's husband, a jovial man with a terrible temper, had almost left her one year, for a girl he kept back in Korea; that Mrs. Kim's husband couldn't hold on to a job to save his life and that their new frozen-yogurt stand at the mall was not financially solvent; that Mrs. Lee and her daughter hadn't spoken in years.

In the meantime, we noticed that Sora's pregnancy had lent her pale, sickly form a beauty we had never seen on her before, rounding her stomach and illuminating her face so that she shone like a sleek pearl. As the months went by, the baby brought a flush to her cheeks, a sheen to her skin, a curl to her eyelashes, and a stately, elegant rhythm to her walk. She began to raise her eyes to ours on Sundays and return our greetings with warmth. She held her head as though it were a bright flower on a stalk, held up high for the world to see, and her hair fanned out behind her in red-gold waves.

"If that's what sin does to you," whispered Mrs. Lee to Mrs. Kim, "then perhaps we could all stand to sin a little more." We ignored Mrs. Lee, who was vain about her looks even now, in her sixties, when her waist had thickened with time and her teeth had yellowed with age, as all of ours had.

But one by one, we noticed that the changes to Sora began to extend to us as well. Mrs. Park's hair grew back, as thick and strong as smooth rope, the color now a mirror-bright gray. Mr. and Mrs. Kim's shop began to attract visitors in droves, people at the mall lining up to taste the cold, sour-sweet coils of frozen yogurt in flavors like peach, apricot, matcha, and raspberry. Mrs. Lee finally patched things up with her daughter Stephanie, and she sent us photos of the two of them meeting for lunch, wearing matching red lipstick. And Mrs. Suh's husband bought her a new Louis Vuitton purse and told her that he would stop seeing the girl in Korea (Mrs. Suh suspected that this was because the girl had abandoned him for a richer lover, but she still carried the purse as tenderly as if it were a newborn or a broken arm).

All the while, Sora's belly continued to grow, and she became more and more beautiful, until she shone like a second sun during services. Even Pastor Mark's normally grating voice grew more resonant and measured when Sora turned her face up to the pulpit during his sermons, her attention coaxing something that approached eloquence from him.

Later, it was Mrs. Kim who said that she had seen Sora and Pastor Mark at the mall, sitting on a bench not far from the frozen-yogurt shop. Sora was silent, her hands folded in her lap, as Pastor Mark, dressed in a polo and jeans, spoke to her. Mrs. Kim couldn't hear what he was saying, but then she saw the way Sora lowered her face slowly into the heels of her hands, like her head had suddenly become too heavy for her.

It clicked into place for her then—why Sora continued coming to church on Sundays even though the entire congregation was abuzz with rumors; why she always sat in the center of the front pew, where she could gaze adoringly up at Pastor Mark; why her father refused to address her pregnancy. He was waiting for Pastor Mark to do the right thing, to marry Sora, to cover up their sin with a white veil and the sound of wedding bells.

Mrs. Kim felt her heart contract when Pastor Mark touched the place between the girl's shoulder blades with the flat of his hand, once, before standing up and walking away. She hurriedly began to assemble a bowl of mango and passion-fruit yogurt with coconut flakes and mochi bits on top for Sora, but soon the line of customers grew too long, and the yogurt she had set aside began to melt, and when she looked back up, Sora had left.

We didn't know how to take this news, how to shift the topography of our own faith accordingly. The more pious among us reminded one another that it was a sin to speculate and gossip about a man of God. The less pious among us wanted to wring Pastor Mark's scrawny neck, while the nosy among us wondered when they would have found time to meet at all, and who would have approached whom first. We could not imagine bumbling Pastor Mark, with his shiny shoes and adult braces, in the role of a seducer. Nor could we picture shy, studious Sora boldly approaching an older man, willfully leading him astray from the path of righteousness.

But when Pastor Mark asked us to bow our heads in prayer that Sunday, none of us did; instead, we stared straight ahead at the pulpit, daring him to open his eyes and see our disapproval. The prayers and psalms that we knew by heart no longer held the same power for us that they had always had before.

Later that evening, we found ourselves strangely excited. We reached for our husbands in the night, much to their surprise, and for the first time in years, we felt joy in the darkness of our bedrooms, our skin lit by the glow of the streetlights outside, the years on our bodies suddenly melting away like wrinkles ironed out by steam.

The next day, our phones did not ring with the chimes of our messages to one another. We did not tell one another about what had happened in the night, the sudden longing that had come over us, the need to have our bodies seen and touched and held, even if it was just by our smelly old husbands, most of whom needed pills to get it up anyway. Perhaps it was that same longing that had driven young Sora into Pastor Mark's arms, against all good sense and better judgment, and could we fault her for it, young and foolish as she was, when it turned out we too were still filled with the same desires?

Three Sundays later, Pastor Mark gave the best sermon he had ever given, and despite our distaste for what he had done, our knowledge of his failings, we were moved. His words were winged

lanterns, flying up into the vaulted ceilings of the church and illuminating our faces with their wisdom. He was transfigured by
the word of God, his chubby, boyish face suddenly lean with
authority and filled with conviction. He spoke of the Lord's endless mercy, the refining fire of His love like a tongue of flame that
would scald us into wholeness if we would only disavow our sins
and repent.

We watched Sora, who sat very still, so still that she looked like
a paper doll. She kept her hands over her belly, perhaps to comfort the baby, or herself. We watched Reverend Chang, whose
eyes, fixed on his daughter, began to fill with tears.

Everyone in the congregation stood up to renounce their sins,
raising their hands toward God—everyone, that is, except for
Sora. We felt compelled to stand in our turn as well, and to babble our sins into a river of sound, confessing our covetousness,
lust, greed, pride, wrath, until we felt emptied, as though we'd
relieved ourselves over and over again, until our insides were
nothing but light and air. When we looked back toward Sora's
spot in the front pew, she was gone. The air still held the imprint
of her body, the shape of a girl.

We found her in the church parking lot, her body bent into
a question mark as she knelt on the asphalt, her water broken.
"The baby," she said when she saw us. "He's coming."

We packed her into Mrs. Lee's SUV and massaged her swollen
ankles. Her skin beaded with sweat as she cried out.

"Should we call someone? Should we call Pastor Mark?"
Mrs. Park asked her.

"No," Sora said, her voice harsh but certain. "No, we don't
need him."

We nodded. The baby would come, father or no. The time for
waiting was over. "Let's go, then," Mrs. Suh said.

Mrs. Lee drove us to the hospital. All around us the world

was silent as we held on to Sora and cradled her. She wriggled like a caught fish and began to moan the dark song of birth that we had all known in our time. We sang it back to her, all talk of sins and repentance forgotten now. We squeezed her hand and felt her squeeze ours, wiped the sweat from her brow, fed her mouthfuls of bottled water, reminded her to breathe. We told her baby that he must make the delivery easy on his mother, that the world was waiting for him to arrive. That he was loved. That we were ready.

The Love Song of the Mexican Free-Tailed Bat

By the time you have finished in your father's study, it is almost
4:00 p.m. Texas is experiencing an unseasonably cold snap this
November, and you are shivering while you tie up old newspapers and water-rippled editions of *Time* and *National Geo-
graphic* for the recycling bins outside. You have been wearing
your father's old puffer vest all day, the ratty one that has down
coming out of it and that your mother always hated, and when
you bury your nose in the collar you don't know what you're
expecting to find, exactly—maybe some remnant of his smell,
the slightly mildewy scent of a man who never let his things sit
in the dryer for long enough—but all you smell is stale coffee.

You have already bundled most of his clothing into donation
bags, but you will put the vest inside your suitcase and, at the end
of your weeklong stay, take it back with you to New York City,
where it will hang for months, untouched, in the closet of your
tiny, overheated apartment, like a reproach. After this week, you
will never wear it again. In fact, you will have forgotten that it

is there until one day in late March, when a guy you sometimes sleep with when you're both bored and single, will find it and put it on as a joke. You will feel a pang of loyalty to the vest and tell him to take it off, in a voice sharper than you had intended. Once he has left your apartment, you will put it into a plastic bag and take it to Goodwill.

You are here in Austin because no one else in your family could be. Your mother, who moved back to Seoul after the divorce—the plane fare from Seoul this time of year is astronomical—and your sister, Joan, married and pregnant in Boston—who is now, as she told you over the phone, "as big as a house that's swallowed another house"—both had reasonable excuses for not being able to come. But the truth is that you are the only one in your family who was on speaking terms with your father before he died, and even now, your mother and your sister do not want to have anything to do with him. So it has fallen on you to travel all the way out to Texas, to pick up the ashes from your father's cremation, and to clean his house, the house you grew up in.

Yesterday, when you got the news—via a voicemail from someone at the university where he had taught biology for the last twenty years—that your father had died of a heart attack at home, alone and surrounded by stacks of research with a single moldy peanut-butter-and-jelly sandwich next to him, you were sure that you'd gotten some bad intel. For one, your father would never have eaten a peanut-butter-and-jelly sandwich, at least not voluntarily. He had always hated peanut butter, didn't like the way it clung to the inside of the mouth like a hug that went on for too long.

When the voicemail notification popped up on your phone, you had been preparing for a meeting with a difficult client. Your boss always gives you the demanding ones, because you have developed a reputation for toughness, that rare ability (at least in a woman, at least according to your boss) to put an important man in his place without offending him. After listening to the voicemail, you stood up, turned your computer off, and went home. You called Joan as soon as you got outside. Then you called your mother as soon as you got home. The next day, you packed a suitcase without seeing anything you put inside it, called a cab to the airport, and got on the first flight to Austin.

Your plane was filled with people who, it seemed, had never learned how to behave in polite society. You gritted your teeth to keep from snapping at the woman who attempted to squeeze her suitcase next to yours in the overhead compartment, and, unable to close the compartment, had to ask at least three people for help before her case was wedged securely inside. The couple sitting next to you—newlyweds, you guessed, from the way the woman was flaunting the giant wedding ring on her finger—kissed ostentatiously and chattered about their trip until you wanted to scream. You had to breathe out through your mouth, your frustration almost paralyzing you, when the man in the seat in front of you leaned his chair back too far and practically landed in your lap. You asked the flight attendant for a glass of wine, which you drank too quickly, and only then did your anger at everyone around you dissipate. You spent the rest of the flight asleep with your mouth open, drool collecting down the side of your chin, like a child or an old woman.

Your visit coincided with the arrival of a pop star for a multi-day stop in the city, and the airport was filled with excited fans wearing T-shirts emblazoned with the pop star's face. You considered buying a T-shirt too, just to feel like you were part of something, and for an instant you thought about getting your father one as well, before remembering he was dead. Then you laughed until you cried while driving out of the airport in your

rental car at the idea of your balding, bespectacled father—
a figure you had feared and revered while growing up but who
couldn't have been more than five foot six in his socks—wearing
tour merch.

Your first stop was your father's office at the university, to
meet with one of his graduate students. You parked crookedly
and waited impatiently for him to show up in the lobby of the
building.

He—a tall white boy with wild flyaway hair and big, unfash-
ionable glasses—was ten minutes late.

"Hi, I'm Benjamin?" he said, like it was a question.

You squinted at him and barely shook the proffered hand. He
was significantly taller than you, but he had a spine like a candy
cane and a slouch so self-effacing that you instantly felt at ease
around him.

"I was the one who called you," he said.

"Right, thanks," you said. "Are those his things?"

He was carrying a cardboard box with several tears in it that
had been patched up with duct tape. He loaded it into your car
and then gave you the house keys. "I hope it's not weird that your
dad gave me those. I used to house-sit for him sometimes."

"How did you know my father again?"

"He was my adviser. I'm writing my thesis on the mating
calls of Mexican free-tailed bats," he said self-consciously, like
you were about to ask him for the abstract. To your horror, he
seemed, for a moment, about to cry. "Your father meant a lot to
me," he said. He gave you his number. "I lost my mom last year,
and I would have given up on my PhD if your father hadn't been
there for me."

You didn't have time to consider the import of what Benjamin
had said until you were in the car again, when you realized that

he had looked up to your father. That, for Benjamin, he was a trusted mentor, someone other than the man you grew up with. The resentment you felt at this stuck in the back of your throat, like peanut butter.

When you got to the house, you were stunned by how familiar it still felt, even though you had not been back in years. All the shades were drawn, except for the one over the window of what used to be your childhood bedroom, which was only half drawn. From the driveway, it looked like the house was slowly winking at you. You turned the ignition off and wiped your sweaty hands on the steering wheel. *They have already taken his body away,* you reminded yourself. But trepidation still knocked against your heart as you fumbled with the house keys and unlocked the door.

Inside, the air was musty. Dirty dishes teetered in the kitchen sink, the crusts of yellow yolk hardened on their rims. There were books, research journals, papers piled on top of almost every available surface. You opened the windows to let in some light and air, and then you saw it, the huge flight cage in the backyard.

You walked outside to inspect it, noticing that the grass was almost as tall as your knees. Your father had constructed the cage himself, out of metal piping and netting, after your mother finally left him. Hanging from the ceiling of the cage like soft Christmas-tree ornaments were small brown balls of fur, the bats your father loved more than anything else in the world.

Most of the bats were sleeping, but one of them opened its eyes when it heard you. It had velvety, petal-like ears, and its upturned nostrils quivered when you approached the cage. It stared at you appraisingly and clicked twice before deciding that you were not a threat.

Bats use their sense of smell to determine who to mate with, to sniff out a partner with the gene pool most divergent from their own. There are studies showing that humans do the same thing, but you have yet to see any evidence in your personal life that the smell test has helped anyone avoid heartbreak or disappointment. Most humans you know, including yourself, are notoriously bad at deciding on a mate.

You wondered what this bat could tell about you from the way you smelled. Could it smell grief? Anger? Love? Or did it detect a heady cocktail of all the above, spiced with notes of your sweat and hormones? Do bats miss the smell of one another when one of them dies?

Here are all the other things you know about these bats: The Mexican free-tailed bat has a wingspan of eleven inches across and the eager, not unadorable face of a pocket gremlin. Its tiny fangs include an upper third molar, which is used for grinding insects. Unlike other bat species, it has a small, free-standing tail extending below its clawed feet, which it uses to navigate. You know these facts like you know that Joan has always wanted to be a mother—unlike you—and that her left eye twitches when she's trying not to cry.

Bats were why your father, as a young physics student at UT Austin, newly arrived in the States from Gwangju, had changed his course of study to the less prestigious field of biology. He loved them, their squashed, doglike faces and their bright, inquisitive eyes. He was the one who told you that, contrary to popular belief, bats actually had wonderful eyesight.

Joan was frightened of bats, screamed on the few occasions when a confused young pup flew into the house by mistake. But your father taught you to love them, and sometimes he took you with him on his research trips to the caves in San Antonio. You would stand next to him, feeling the damp chill of the wet cave walls, breathing in the funk of the bats, while listening to them click in the dark. "Goddamn tourists," your father muttered whenever he found cigarette butts or crushed beer cans in the dirt.

"You and your appa are two of a kind," your mother used to say when you were little, shaking her head. At first you liked the idea of being similar to your father, who you thought was the smartest person in the world, but as time went on it became clear that this was not always a good thing. Your father was a difficult, prickly man, prone to bouts of rage that seemed to appear out of nowhere. As a child, you became well versed in reading the ever-shifting weather patterns of his moods, and you learned how to tiptoe around the landmines of his outbursts.

When you entered your teens, you learned how to marshal your anger whenever you became the target of his rage, to raise your voice against his bellow until it felt like the windows of the house would shatter. You had epic fights: about the right way to parallel-park a car; your first boyfriend, whom your father frightened so badly the first time you brought him home that he tried to break up with you the next day; the fact that you wanted to go to NYU instead of the university in town. But he was strangely proud of you, proud of what he called your fearlessness and inability to be daunted.

Even now, you are at times awestruck by the power of your own anger, which can seem like an ungovernable force of nature— a storm spinning out of control and leaving broken dinner plates and cracked phone screens in its wake. At times, you are not sure where your anger ends and your father's begins.

It is fashionable now to talk about angry women, how great

it is to be a woman and actually get to show anger. What is not so fashionable is to be the kind of woman who gets angry about the wrong things or in the wrong way. And, of course, what no one talks about is that not all women get to be angry in the same ways.

You are five foot three and thirty-four years old, and you have the kind of face that means you will probably be carded well into your forties. A blessing, your white friends moan. But looking younger than you actually are has significant drawbacks, especially when it comes to having your anger taken seriously. And when it is taken seriously, you are rarely forgiven.

Six months ago, after you threw his phone across the room during an argument, your last boyfriend, Jeff, had told you that you needed to start seeing someone about what he called your anger issues. That it wasn't normal for someone to be so upset all the time, that it had become difficult to be around you. You had tried to argue with this, saying that there was nothing wrong with you or your anger. In fact, you wanted to tell him, your anger had actually served you well in life, at least professionally. At work—this January, you will have been working at your law firm for five years—you have successfully managed to bend and hammer the molten, white-hot anger you so often feel at your clueless male boss and colleagues into a shiny, hard alloy that you use to shield yourself. "The Terminator," they call you in the office, and part of you loves it.

But you didn't say any of that, because you knew that he was right. That something inside you had broken and bent a little too far over the years in the service of your anger and was now perhaps beyond repair. And instead of admitting it, and saying you were sorry, and asking him to stay, you told him to get out of your apartment and your life.

Your father probably would have done the same thing, you think now as you drag the garbage bins out to the curb. He could never admit when he was wrong, or when he was suffering.

Once, when you were in high school, your father got into a fight with another man in the school parking lot, after he came to pick you up from debate club. The man—who was another student's father—pointed out that your father had scratched the side of his car. After about two minutes of an increasingly heated back-and-forth, your father had begun shouting and threatening to hit the other man. You were in tears, trying to hold his arms back and begging him to stop, because everyone else in the parking lot was staring at the spectacle the three of you made. But he did not hear you, and no one came to help, and finally the other man got back into his car and drove away.

Later, in the driveway in front of your house, your father killed the engine and turned toward you. "Don't tell your mother about this," he said quietly. "Now go on inside."

But twenty, thirty minutes later, your father was still in the car, and when you went back outside to check on him, you saw that he was crying, his shoulders shaking and his head bent over the steering wheel. You were frightened then in a way that you had never been at his rages, at the notion that the same man who could come to blows with a stranger over something as inconsequential as a scratch could weep like a child afterward.

It's 6:20 p.m. now, the sky just beginning to darken. You get into your rental car and circle the neighborhood for a place to eat, but you find yourself driving downtown, toward Congress Avenue Bridge. You've come here so many times before with your father, to watch the bats that live on this bridge launch themselves into the moist velvet of the night sky to hunt. It was one of his favorite things, and soon it became one of yours too—the sight of more than a million bats, many of them pups only a few months old, pouring out from the bridge and along the tree line, like a second river, suspended in the air.

You park your car near a gas station and walk the rest of the way to the bridge, where a small crowd has already gathered. A child of about nine or ten is whining to her mother. "I'm bored," she says. "I want to go back to the hotel and watch cartoons."

You stiffen and wait for the mother to grow impatient, to snap at the child, to threaten her with some dire, unspecified punishment if she doesn't behave herself. But she doesn't, and something inside you expands with relief. The woman simply reaches into her purse to hand her daughter a bag of fruit snacks and tousles her hair. "Try to be patient, okay? It's worth it, I promise," she says. You wonder if this is the type of mother Joan will be, unlike your mother, whose difficult marriage often made her neurotic and unforgiving toward you both. You remember flinching whenever you or Joan spilled or dropped something in the kitchen, how your mother, obsessed with cleanliness, would immediately scold both of you, no matter who did it. Sometimes, when she was in a mood, the scolding would go on and on until it became the rageful refrain of her favorite song, "None of You Appreciate Me and It Would Serve This Family Right If I Stopped Doing the Innumerable Things I Do for All of You Without Being Asked," or another favorite, "If You Have to Ask Me Why I'm Mad, You Don't Deserve to Know." All this and more, over a glass of spilled orange juice, a bent fork tine, a dish washed improperly.

You remember your father telling you, when you were little, that the bats that live on this bridge are mostly mothers and their babies. The adult males lived in bachelor colonies, he told you, not too far away. "Why do they live away from their families?" you had asked. "They're probably happier that way," your father said, and you had felt a coldness steal through your chest, like a small bat inside your rib cage had placed one leathery wing gently against your heart. You had wondered for years afterward if your father would have been happier without you, no longer part of the colony of your family.

The sky is a soft periwinkle, lit by the yellow wink of street-lights, by the time the first of the bats, the scouts, come out. A hush runs through the crowd, and even the traffic seems to still. The bats stream down the shorelines and around the trees, moving so quickly that it makes you dizzy to keep your eye on any one of them for very long.

Summer was your father's favorite time for watching the bats fly out from the bridge, when the dry heat drove them out before dark and they came careening out so thickly that you couldn't even see the buildings on the other side of the river. When the hot sun tipped their fur with gold, and they looked like a symphony, a spiral staircase, a dark rainbow.

You stand, face turned up to the sky until the back of your neck hurts, watching the bats head east, down the river, out to the farms and hills on the outskirts of the city.

Once the last of the bats have disappeared into the night, you call Benjamin and ask him to meet you at a bar near the university, the kind that has darts and dirty pitchers of beer. You used to go there all the time when you were in college and home on breaks, until you stopped coming home for breaks.

Your father never forgave you for going away to college, especially to a place like NYU, when you could have gone to the university here for free. But you wanted to get out of Austin, to go east to a place where it snowed and seasons actually meant something. You wanted to try to leave your family—and the long shadow of your father—behind.

Benjamin shows up looking even more disheveled than he did earlier. You've already had two whiskeys by the time he arrives, and your joints feel warm and loose. "So tell me about the mating calls of Mexican free-tailed bats," you say as he stares into his beer glass. His eyes light up like you've given him a present, and he spends the next twenty minutes telling you all about his research. He shows you the audio files on his phone, at least a year's worth of recordings of horny bats. He tells you that male bats sing in patterns, repeating the same phrases to attract females.

"They're love songs, kind of," he says, blushing. Apparently, it is rare to see this kind of patterned, syntactical vocal communication in animals other than birds and whales.

It is clear that Benjamin idolizes your father. He rhapsodizes about your father's brilliance and patience with his students, even the anxious, overeager freshmen in his introductory biology classes who have nervous breakdowns over every lab and exam. You get drunk and smile at all the right parts and concentrate on not falling off your stool, until the glass bottles over the bar also seem to be smiling back at you and this version of your father—the generous, attentive man who genuinely loved teaching and imparting wisdom to young people—almost seems real.

At the end of the night, you ask him to give you a ride back home. "It would be irresponsible of you to let me drive back like this," you slur in what you hope is a flirtatious manner. "Yes, it would," he responds dryly.

His car is, predictably, a Prius with a Greenpeace bumper

sticker. There are several empty soda cans and stacks of books in the back, along with what you think are a few apple cores. On the drive home, you try to guess how old he is. His lack of style and general eagerness to please seem to suggest that he is somewhere in his mid- to late twenties, but the lines around his eyes and the cautious way he turns corners and changes lanes indicate that he is perhaps older than you initially thought. He laughs when you ask him.

"I guess I probably seem like a mess to you," he says, gesturing at the back seat.

"Not a mess, just messy," you say. "You just need a haircut, is all." He laughs again. You are grateful to have something resembling a friend here, in this city that has never felt like home, even if it is just for this one night. Even if he is only being nice to you because he feels sorry for you.

Outside the house, you tell him that you need him to come see something with you. You take him out back, stumbling a little, to where the flight cage is. The bats chitter when they see you, and you tell them to hush, like they are naughty children.

"Well?" you say to Benjamin. "What am I supposed to do with them?"

"Feed them," he says. He disappears into the garage for a while, and then emerges with a bucket of fat, golden mealworms. You watch, both repelled and fascinated, as he opens the flight cage door, closes it behind him, and feeds each bat. They eat with a shuddering, ferocious devotion that moves you, their tiny faces becoming mostly jaws and teeth as they bite down on each doomed worm. Their hunger, the black-and-white equation of it, reminds you how easy it is to love something when its needs are so simple.

Back in the house, you make Benjamin wash his hands, and

then you ask him to play you one of his recordings. He puts his phone inside a mug from the kitchen, to amplify the sound. The two of you sit in the dimly lit living room and listen to the trills and whirs of bats in love. You close your eyes, and instantly you are transported back to girlhood, when you would walk through the caves with your father and listen to what sounded like a private orchestra, millions of tiny flutes and kazoos, whistling and buzzing away in an endless series of ripples.

When you open your eyes, Benjamin is staring at you with the kind of tenderness you have not seen in what feels like years. You don't think anyone has looked at you like this since Jeff, who, when you came down with a bad cold last year, was appalled that you had never taken a sick day and made you stay home and drink bowl after bowl of his grandmother's chicken soup, which he made himself in your tiny kitchen. The smell of dill and chicken fat still fills your mouth with watery regret.

You lead Benjamin upstairs, to what used to be your childhood bedroom, and you fumble at his shirt buttons while he fumbles with the zipper of your jeans. You place your hand on top of his and guide him, and when you come, it is with a force so startling that it makes you cry, and he strokes your hair before falling asleep. You lie awake for what seems like hours, listening to the song of the bats filling the house.

You consider the possibility that Jeff's willingness to care for you was at the root of why you had reacted so poorly when he told you your anger was untenable for him. You had foolishly allowed yourself to make a home in him, and as a result, his concern had stung more than if he had shoved you against a bookshelf and called you a crazy bitch. That was a language you understood. You had grown up telling yourself that your father's rage came from love, even when it didn't feel that way.

That sometimes love curdled into a solution so volatile it erupted into overturned chairs, books thrown across a hallway, or words that nestled deep inside you and lay dormant for years until they had braided themselves into your DNA. Displays of anger were a by-product of love, you had always thought, until Jeff told you otherwise. The idea that love could also manifest in telling someone else that it was not your job to hold their anger, to receive it like a kiss, had never occurred to you before.

One time, when you were twelve and Joan was fourteen, your father got into an argument with her while driving you both home from school. Joan wanted a ride to the mall that Saturday, but your father told her that she would need to get a perfect score on an upcoming science test in order to go. When Joan muttered that if he would bother helping her with her homework—instead of just yelling at her about it all the time—maybe she'd have a chance of passing the test, or even getting a hundred, your father had become so angry that he had stopped the car on the side of the road and leaned across Joan to open the passenger door. You were only about two miles away from home, but the road was relatively busy, without many sidewalks. It was a stiflingly hot September day. Lines of heat rose from the asphalt.

You saw Joan's left eye twitch in the rearview mirror. "I'm sorry," she said to your father. The radio was playing classical music, something soothing with strings that sounded more suited to a dentist's office than as the soundtrack for whatever bad thing was about to happen now.

"Get out of the car," he said.

"I said, I'm sorry," she said, a rising note of panic in her voice. Other cars drove by, unconcerned with your family's little drama. The only sound inside the car was your fast, shallow breathing and the whirring of the air conditioner. After a few more seconds, Joan unbuckled her seatbelt and slid out of the car. "I hate you," she said to your father in a low voice while you watched from the back seat, the blood gone from your face.

You waited for your father to relent, to tell Joan to get back in the car and for things to go back to normal. It was ninety-seven degrees outside. Sweat trickled down the back of your neck, and your thighs were stuck to the leather car seat. But no one said anything, and your father drove away in a cloud of dust, running two red lights.

"Where's Joan?" your mother asked when you got home, before she saw the look on your father's face and the tears on yours. Your father went upstairs to his study, slamming the door, and your mother retreated to the kitchen without a word. You followed her and watched as she cut up plums and nectarines (Joan's favorite), listening to the thwack of the blade against the cutting board.

Almost an hour later, Joan knocked on the front door and you let her in. You brought her a glass of water and the plate of fruit, and in the cool darkness of your shared bedroom, you tried to talk to her, to comfort her by saying useless things, like "You know how he gets," while she stared straight up at the ceiling and finally told you to save it. She and your father did not speak for months.

Another time, your father and mother fought at the airport, on the way back from a family vacation. They sat side by side at the gate, arguing furiously in low voices over something you didn't understand. You were trying to bury yourself in a *Cosmo* magazine you had secretly bought for the flight when you saw, all at once, your father swing his hand back to strike your mother's face and then stop, midair. Joan was in the bathroom, so no one but you saw your mother's eyes go blank, as though she had flown out of her own body. And you, seventeen then, began to love your father a little less.

The last time you went with your father on a cave expedition, you were ten and you got horribly lost. One minute, it seemed, you were walking beside your father, making the beam of your flashlight dance on the walls, and the next minute, when you had stopped to admire a particularly complicated arrangement of stalagmites, he was gone. You weren't scared at first, because you could hear his footsteps from what sounded like just a few yards ahead in the yawning dark. It was only when you continued to walk farther into the cave without seeing him that you became frightened.

"Appa?" you called. Your voice echoed, reverberating through the hollows and furrows of rock.

Your father had a habit of striding ahead of you and the rest of your family, no matter where you were, that drove your mother crazy. Even when you went on vacation, he would walk at a pace that you and your sister, especially as children, could hardly keep up with. "It's like you're *trying* to lose us," your mother would say to him. But you had never been left behind all by yourself before.

You sat down on a rock and waited to be found, trying to be sensible. But when the beam of your flashlight began to stutter, you started to cry, wondering what would happen if no one ever came for you. Just then, you heard him, calling your name. You shouted back, and his voice, brittle with relief, came bouncing off the cave walls. He tried to get you to describe where you were, but your head was swimming with panic and you could barely speak.

There was a silence. And then: "Santoki, tokiya." Your father was singing. You dried your tears, astonished. You had not heard him sing in years, not since you were young enough to request lullabies and bedtime stories. "Santoki," a children's song about a mountain rabbit, had always been your favorite.

"Santoki, tokiya," you sang back, your voice quavering. You followed the sound of your father's voice, your voices becoming louder and clearer as you drew nearer to each other, singing all the while.

When you finally found him, in a chamber not far from the mouth of the cave, you braced yourself for his anger, the yelling, the flood of recriminations. But, instead, he dropped to his knees and held you tight, squashing your face into his shoulder while he thanked, again and again, a God you had not even known he believed in.

The next morning, you wake up before Benjamin does, your mouth dry and sour from the whiskey. You throw on your father's vest, shuffle on your sneakers, and walk outside, head pounding. The sun is just beginning to rise, and the light is a white-gold that streaks through the tree branches.

Inside the flight cage, the bats are roosting, but they stir at your approach. You think about the first time you ever got to see a bat up close, how your father's voice was a reverent whisper as he explained to you that baby bats, despite being the size of cashews and completely hairless, are born with strong legs and claws so they can hang on tight to their mothers. They are flightless for the first few weeks of their lives, and if they fall, they will die. You think about the fact that almost every living thing starts off small and helpless. It seems miraculous to you that anything survives growing up.

You unlatch the flight cage and stand outside it, waiting. One brave bat stretches its wings toward the open door, and then slips out into the morning air. The other bats seem hesitant, but then they follow the first bat, their wings jittery and dappled with sunlight, chirping softly to one another. Despite your hangover, you find that your heart soars with the bats as they take to the air, climbing up its currents and pathways. You think about the many contradictions of bats—that they are the only mammals that can fly, their ability to divine direction in darkness, their need for one another despite a preference for solitude.

Then they are all gone, except for one lone bat on the ground. The bat looks stunned, as though it has just woken up and forgotten where it is. You run back inside for a dish towel and use it to gently pick the bat up. There is a small tear in one of the fine membranes of its wings.

Your father told you that the wings of a bat are actually its hands, each veined segment a bony, elongated finger with leathery webbing stretched across. He had shown you how they use their wings like hands, flying through the air the way a swimmer pulls herself through water.

"What happened, little guy?" you ask. Its eyes are so intelligent and alert that you almost expect it to answer you. Its enormous ears swivel with your every breath, and it hooks its thumbs into the folds of the towel, as if it is thrusting itself upward to get a better look at you.

That sun-streaked morning, you tell yourself two things. Someday, you will forgive your father, and you will remember his occasional tenderness and be able to hold it alongside the hurt he caused you and your family and see it all like light through a prism, refracted by both the things you cannot look at and the things you cannot look away from.

Even though you know that it is pointless, and in fact quite dangerous, as your father would say, to anthropomorphize animals, you feel as though the bat is looking up at you as if to say, "Where to next?" And because of this, and because you and the bat are both far from home—wherever that might be for either of you—you open your mouth and you sing to it.

Acknowledgments

Thank you to my friends, many of whom are also my first readers: Vanessa Chan, Katie Devine, Daniel Gibney, Grace Shuyi Liew, Kate Tooley, and Jemimah Wei.

Thank you to my teachers, who read and helped shape many of these stories in their first forms: Marie-Helene Bertino, K-Ming Chang, Ann Hood, Mira Jacob, and Wayétu Moore.

Thank you to my agent, Danielle Bukowski, for her invaluable support and for believing in me and these stories.

Thank you to my editor, Caitlin Landuyt, for her brilliant edits and insights into all things astrological and beyond.

Thank you to the whole Vintage team for their incredible work and for giving my books a beautiful home: Nick Alguire, Steve Walker, Eddie Allen, Abby Endler, Suzanne Herz, Anna Noone, Austin O'Malley, Quinn O'Neill, Madeline Partner, Barbara Richard, Jordan Rodman, and Melissa Yoon.

Thank you to my family: Kwang-Hyun Chung, Soonhee Chung, and Yuna Chung.

Thank you to Emily Jungmin Yoon for graciously allowing me to use the last lines of your poem "Say Grace" (from *A Cruelty Special to Our Species*, Ecco, 2018) in the epigraph of this book.

Thank you to all the journals that first published some of these stories—*Catapult, F(r)iction, Gulf Coast, The Idaho Review, Indiana Review, The Kenyon Review, One Story, Pleiades, Split Lip, VIDA Review, Waxwing, Wigleaf*—and to the editors who worked with me on them: Leah Johnson, Mia Herman, Dani Hedlund, Helen Maimaris, Katie Edkins Milligan, Natanya Biskar, Mitch Wieland, Laura Dzubay, Shreya Fadia, Kirsten Reach, Will Allison, Patrick Ryan, Jennifer Maritza McCauley, Michele Finn Johnson, Maureen Langloss, Grace Johnson, Naomi Krupitsky, Feliz Moreno, K-Ming Chang, Rose Skelton, and Scott Garson.

Thank you to the Asian American Writers' Workshop, the Center for Fiction, Kweli, the New School, Sevilla Writers House, and Tin House, where many of these stories first began.

Thank you to all the storytellers of my life.